Big Guy and Devereaux
A Father and Son's Journey on the
Back Roads of the Heart.

By C.M. Benefield

Pleasant View Publishing
Terrebonne, Oregon

Pleasant View Publishing
Terrebonne, Oregon

Acknowledgement

This book explores the relationships that exist within a family. It served to bring closure to the relationship that I had with my father, a unique man who touched the lives of many people. I wish to thank my wife Lorri Benefield for all her love and support in the editing of this book and in our travels together.

C. M. Benefield
Terrebonne, Oregon
December 3, 2015

*This book is dedicated to my father Devereaux Joseph Benefield,
and all of those souls who choose "the path less taken".*

CONTENTS

Chapters

ISBN-10: 978-0-692-82192-9
ISBN-13: 978-0-692-82192-3

Published by Pleasant View Publishing, Terrebonne, Oregon

Chapter 1

It Was a Blessed Life in Both Time and Place.

After a turbulent war between the generations, Devereaux and his youngest son, "Big Guy", were fortunate enough to travel together along the back roads of the American West. Like those forgotten roads, the contours of one generation adapt to accommodate the next within the topography of time. This is the story of one such landscape, a common topography that brought the lives of a father and son together to explore the roads both taken and ignored.

Devereaux Meehan was born in 1922, in a house that his father built on Cerritos Avenue in Long Beach, California. He said that a veterinarian had brought him into the world, in the kitchen on the dining room table. Whatever the case, his parents were somewhat surprised that he had arrived at all.

Devereaux was the last of five children in the Meehan house, a handful of boisterous energy who grew to manhood through the depths of the Great Depression. He was a curious and energetic boy, who busied himself around the neighborhood collecting junk, until his mother found him a job selling magazines and umbrellas on the beach.

Devereaux came from a family that had settled a continent and had fought in every war in American history. The promise of America had shaped this family; taken them from ignorance and hard times and delivered them to a blessed life in both time and place.

From the wreckage of the Civil War, Devereaux's great grandfather, had died as a homeless, disabled union veteran, who left a family that was forced to travel west. With only Devereaux's grandfather and his great uncle to support the family of five, they struggled to survive the turbulent times in a lawless West. From farm laborers to machinists who toiled for the railroads, the Meehan's forged a better life, as they built the next railroad that tied the West to the rest of the Union. From Indiana through Kansas where they buried their mother, to the wilds of eastern Oregon and finally to the golden shores of Southern California the Meehan's finally settled down to create a place for themselves, that was free of the turmoil that had pursued them.

The Southern California of the early 1920s was a sunny and carefree paradise, especially down at the seashore. Devereaux grew up by the sea and was a proficient swimmer and body surfer. He had spent many days camping and hunting in the open spaces that existed long before the land gave way to endless housing tracts and congested freeways. Devereaux spoke of duck hunting with his dad in the marsh at Bolsa Chica. Bolsa Chica was then a waving sea of grass where the sky darkened in the fall and spring as large flocks of sea birds passed over head. Devereaux always laughed when he recalled the time when he and a friend were cooking a rabbit over a tumbleweed campfire in the middle of a J.P. Getty oil field, back in 1932. The boys were just about to eat when a gust of wind sent one of the burning tumbleweeds rolling into a waste oil pond. This started a chain of events and a raging oilfield fire that burned for a couple of weeks. Devereaux and his friend ran for their lives and carried the secret with them for the rest of their days.

In 1933, when Devereaux was 11 years old, an earthquake destroyed most of Long Beach, including every school in town. Devereaux spent the next year attending school in a large tent, when he wasn't standing in line for relief supplies of bread and canned milk. 1933 was a bad year for a disaster, as the world itself had become one big disaster by then. But the Meehan's survived as they always had, through hard work and a hard fought faith forged by earlier disasters.

Devereaux had always been a character. He had established himself as a hardworking, dedicated, and trustworthy man. He used to say; "My faith, my country and my union." These constituted the core beliefs of Devereaux. Somewhere in the mix was his family; interwoven within the fabric of this man, who seemed to love living more deeply than most. His father before him had been a union electrician, and was one of the founders of the International Brotherhood of Electrical Workers (IBEW), Local 711 in the City of Long Beach. The Meehans were blue collar to their core; their hands were the instruments of their success, as much as their determination to persevere had been.

In keeping with his character, Devereaux left many memorable and unique examples of what religion and politics meant to him. He did not trust the rich and powerful and would rail against unelected power and small town politics whenever he had the chance. Devereaux had a lively and hilarious sort of wisdom that resonated within his family.

After Devereaux returned from the South Pacific, where he served in the U.S. Navy during the Second World War, he met Priscilla at a dance at Saint Anthony High School. Priscilla had just left the Immaculate Heart Convent where she had spent the last year studying to be a nun. During that time, she had decided that her greatest purpose in life was to have a family instead of pursuing the cloistered life of a nun. Several months after the dance, in the summer of 1947 Devereaux and Priscilla were married. Their relationship could be described as if Mother Theresa had met Archie Bunker. They were indeed the odd couple-complete opposites. In spite of their differences, their core values were a mirror image of each other. Fifty years of marriage only served to strengthen their bond.

Devereaux was a construction electrician, who worked hard to feed his family. He was working on a supermarket in the rapidly expanding suburbs of Los Angeles when he heard, "Hey Benny!" A fellow electrician shouted into the attic of the unfinished warehouse, "You need to come down otta there, your wife is here and she says that it's time." Three hours later on that Veterans Day in 1958, at Saint Mary's hospital in Long Beach, Big Guy was born. It was the first time that Devereaux and Big Guy met. But then again when does a son really see his father for the very first time? The Meehans now totaled six kids.

Being that he was the baby and the youngest of five boys and a sister, Big Guy was considered the lucky one. He grew up with a different sense of Devereaux than his older siblings. It is said that the youngest within a family always enjoys a special relationship with their parents. Big Guy's brothers and sister knew this and were always chiding him for being "The favorite son". However, each child was the product of a working class Catholic family. Born of Scots and Irish descent; each family member including Sheila, learned to fight at a young age. The Meehan's were proud of whom they were, and while they fought amongst themselves, God help anyone who threatened any one of them. This was especially handy for the youngest member of the Meehan Clan. Perhaps Big Guy was indeed the favorite son.

In later years on Sundays during the summer, Devereaux would load up Priscilla and the kids and they would drive to Sunset Beach and spend the day. Big Guy could remember watching Devereaux body surf the waves effortlessly; steering his husky frame as though the waves had transformed him into a marine mammal. Big Guy was all of four years old when Devereaux picked him up and carried him far out into the surf. As he held Big Guy tight and they bobbed around in the cool ocean, Devereaux was treading water and waiting for the next wave. As the waves approached, he tossed Big Guy up into the air

over the incoming wave and caught him once
again. Within the exhilaration of that moment
so long ago, unknown at the time, Devereaux
was teaching his son about the importance of
trust. In his strong arms, Big Guy was safe and
through Devereaux's example, he learned to
tempt the tides.

Sunday's were also the times when the
family would have a big family dinner,
complete with roast beef, mashed potatoes,
gravy and peas. Sunday was when Devereaux's
mother, Ethel would join the family for dinner.
Grandma Ethel was the daughter of Irish
immigrants. Raised in a mining camp in the
Arizona Territory during the latter 1880s, Ethel
had always enjoyed reciting poetry and singing
little ditties, a trait that she had passed onto her
youngest son Devereaux. Why the name
Devereaux you might ask? It was the name of
one of the heroes of a traveling Wild West
show- "Devero the Montana Scout". It was
also Devereaux's father's middle name.
Devereaux's Aunt Nell suggested that the
spelling change to reflect its French origins.
The name was a blessing and a curse to
Devereaux, but it stuck and was always a
challenge to spell.

Gathered around the dinner table, the family
would listen to Grandma Ethel tell stories
from a different time and place, stories of

hardship and good versus evil from the depths of the wild American West.

"Tell us about the wild cows grandma", a young voice would ask from somewhere beyond the peas.

"Oh yes- the wild longhorns!" Grandma Ethel replied, her dark eyes piercing back to the far reaches of her memory.

"I was just a little girl and I was going to fetch water at the well with my two dogs, Prince and Rover. Suddenly as I came around the bushes toward the well, there was a large longhorn bull standing by the well.

The bull snorted and stamped his feet and I was scared to death that he would attack. Those longhorns were wild and vicious back in those days you know. So anyhow, I stood my ground and then I yelled "Sick em Prince- Sick em Rover!" Both my dogs rushed the bull and I ran back home as fast as I could!" Grandma Ethel said with wide eyes, as she grit her teeth and smiled.

"What happened to the dogs?" Sheila asked. "Oh they came back home all right."

Grandma Ethel replied.

Grandma Ethel was a hard woman who had lived a hard life; yet there was within her something gentle and sweet. She possessed a sense of wild refinement and resilience. Like a cactus flower in the harshness of the desert, to her life was a beautiful thing that survived in spite of all that oppressed it. She was tough and sweet because those were the most important qualities that life in the desert of the Arizona Territory had taught her.

It was a Meehan Family trait to confer a nickname to everyone and sometimes several to the same individual- depending upon the circumstances. Big Guy had several bestowed upon him- for better or for worse. To his siblings Big Guy was known as "Gorgo the Monster", or "Gore" for short. This name originated from the Sunday horror films, which were prevalent during his youth. Gorgo was a giant Japanese mutant lizard who, like Godzilla, brought destruction upon Tokyo. Big Guy would line up objects like shoes, which to him were the surrogates of automobiles and other toys that he lacked at that time. Big Guy would proceed to stomp around on them like Gorgo during those Sunday afternoon matinees in the front room of the Meehan house, where Devereaux would treat the family to root beer floats or apple cider. There was an order to life in those days, a regularity in which the world conformed without question.

To Devereaux, Big Guy was often known as "Piggies" or as "the Birdie" and finally later in life as simply "Big Guy". As a child sitting on Devereaux's big lap, Big Guy remembered

Devereaux singing some obscure piece of poetry, while bouncing him around. Then there was the "oven ritual"; in which if he happened to wander into the kitchen at just the right time, Devereaux would snatch Big Guy up into his arms and pretend as if he was going to toss him into the oven for baking. All the while singing, "I'm going to eat up the Birdie", as Big Guy squealed with delight.

In the heart of this provider and protector there was also the dark side of a complex man; a wild and scary side that Big Guy and his brothers had learned to fear above all else. It would rise to the surface whenever they broke the rules, or allowed his or her wild nature within to show. That dark side would blaze in Devereaux's dark eyes whenever he would discover that someone was not being true to the fundamentals of the values that he and Priscilla had set for the family. Devereaux's voice thundered and roared when he was angry. The Meehan children always depended upon their mother to intercede on their behalf, gladly accepting a spanking with the belt from their mom any time to the wrath of Devereaux.

On one occasion Big Guy's oldest brother, Steve was playing with bows and arrows in the front yard with his friend Terry. Terry had convinced Steve that the rubber tips on the arrows were interfering with their fun. Terry's arrows soon ended up without rubber tips and sharpened into fine pointed missiles. It did not take Devereaux long to discover the danger that was flying around his front yard, as one of the arrows lodged in the lawn next to the porch he was sitting on.

"What in the hell is this!?" Devereaux roared. "Steve, get the hell over here- and bring Terry." Devereaux yelled.

In a flash, Steve came running with Terry in tow. Now being that they were both 7 years old, they instinctively knew that Old Man Meehan was not happy and they may have even been able to deduct the reason for his anger before they stood in front of him. However, Steve did not prepare himself for the dark lightning that blazed in his father's eyes. Fortunately, for Steve he had handed all of the sharpened arrows back to Terry.

"What do you have there Terry?" Devereaux asked in a sarcastic tone that boiled with contempt. It was a tone that came from somewhere in the dark side of his nature. The side of Devereaux that none of his children ever wanted to see out in the open.

"These are my arrows that my dad got me for my birthday." Terry Replied.

"Can I see those?" Devereaux asked with a hiss.

"Sure here you go." Terry replied as he handed the sharpened arrows to Devereaux.

As soon as Devereaux had all the arrows in his hands, he proceeded to snap them like twigs into pieces no longer than 6 inches. Then he handed them back to Terry and said, "Now bring your dad here and I will do the same to him."

Terry and Steve backed off and as Terry turned and ran away in terror, Steve ran into the house to hide under his bed. Devereaux was on the warpath and Big Guy's brothers and sister cleared the area as fast as they could. Fortunately Priscilla came back home from getting her hair done just in time to smooth the situation.

"Pris!" Devereaux bellowed.

"These damn kids have been playing with sharpened arrows. They could have put someone's eye out!" Devereaux yelled.

Priscilla could see "that look" in Devereaux's eyes and was prepared to diffuse the situation. Like a bomb squad member on assignment, Priscilla dissected the situation and rendered Devereaux's temper inert.

"What's that?" Priscilla asked as she pointed at the colored bits of wood laying in the yard.

"Those were Terry's arrows. He won't be putting anyone's eyes out today. I told him to bring his dad over and I would do the same thing to him!" Devereaux replied in anger.

"Oh Devereaux you didn't!" Priscilla said in exasperation.

"Imagine some asshole letting their kids run around with sharpened arrows!" Devereaux replied.

"You just settle down and I will talk with Terry's mom." Priscilla answered.

Terry's father never did show up that day.

Soon Devereaux headed out into the yard to pick up leaves and "let off some steam." Whenever Devereaux got into a bad mood, he would always wander into the yard to water or pick up leaves- one by one, both tasks done by hand. He had a sprinkler system; however he never used it when he was angry.

Big Guy recalled a day in October when he should have been too young to remember those dangerous days which served to define us all. It was a Saturday, but it proved to be different than all the Saturday's that came before it. Devereaux and Priscilla were watching TV on the black and white Packard Bell that occupied its sacred spot in the living room. As Big Guy peeked around the corner of Devereaux's easy chair he saw that President Kennedy was talking on TV. The President ended his speech and the news came on. Big Guy gazed at the Packard Bell as black and white attack jets catapulted from the decks of aircraft carriers and warships plied some far away ocean. After dinner Priscilla called the whole family into the living room and announced that all would kneel down and pray. Big Guy was used to saying a prayer at the dinner table or on Sunday at Mass, but Saturday night was a strange time to have to pray. As the Meehan's said the Rosary that night in 1962, Big Guy began to notice that something was wrong; he could see it on his parent's faces and in the way they prayed. His mother was worried and Big Guy didn't know why. Why was she worried and why did his parents watch the President on TV so intently? Big Guy and his siblings didn't understand the full implications of that Saturday night; nor the fact that it could have been the last Saturday night of their lives were it not for wisdom and the restraint of world leaders and some Russian Submarine officer named Vasili.

When not confronted with global annihilation, Big Guy spent his days roaming the neighborhood as the youngest member of those "Meehan Family Hoodlums." Whether it was climbing on the backyard fence, looking for treasure on garbage pick-up day or initiating an avocado war down the street; Big Guy always found time to get into trouble- just like his older brothers. When school let out in

June, Big Guy would take off his shoes and with the exception of Sunday Mass, his shoes would stay off until summer ended in September. Big Guy's best friend was Johnny Milner, a freckled faced, red haired kid who had one major thing in common with Big Guy- his love for new adventures. Fences didn't stop Big Guy and Johnny from exploring the neighborhood. They challenged each other to see how far down the street they could travel- walking on top of the neighbor's backyard fences. Along the way they would sample the various fruits that happened to be in season and were within reach of the fence.

One day Big Guy and his friend Johnny were playing with Johnnies' dad's golf clubs in his backyard on the corner. Johnny was showing Big Guy how the golf pro Arnold Palmer would use a 7 iron if he were standing there in his backyard. "Don't get too close", Johnny said as Big Guy leaned forward to better see the golf ball. Not heeding his friend's advice, Big Guy continued to gaze at the ball. Before he knew it, Big Guy felt a blunt, stinging pain radiating from the top of his head as Johnny swung the golf club. Not understanding what had happened, Johnny began to laugh as he saw Big Guy began to dance around holding his head. Big Guy started to cry in pain as a blood began to stream down the side of his head. Big Guy then ran home as Johnny, realizing the full gravity of the injury that he had accidentally inflicted upon his friend, followed him. Halfway home, Big Guy ran past Stanley David, who was sitting on his porch eating an apple. As Johnny followed, Stanley asked Johnny what the problem was. Johnny just kept running without saying a word. When Big Guy entered the house, his mother seeing the blood asked what had happened to him. Big Guy cried out, "I was playing golf with Johnny!"

To this Priscilla replied, "Get your head over the sink!"

As she washed the blood off of Big Guy's head, she discovered that the cut was just a minor wound in which she applied hydrogen peroxide, shaved some of the hair away and applied a band aid. All that Johnny saw through the Meehan kitchen window was the blood being washed from Big Guy's head. Johnny started to cry as he ran back toward his house on the corner. Johnny once again passed Stanley David who was by this time heading to the Meehan house to see what all the commotion was about.

"What's wrong Johnny?" Stanley asked.

With tears streaming down his face Johnny replied, "I hit Big Guy in the head with a golf club and it's bloody all over!" Then Johnny turned and ran home. The next day Big Guy and Johnny were back in the backyard shooting baskets as if nothing had happened. Big Guy never had a desire to play golf after that.

One day Big Guy was sitting on the curb floating leaves down the gutter, when Devereaux arrived home from work. Devereaux was dirty and tired as he crawled out of an old Willys panel truck that served as his daily transportation, complements of Hoff Electric.

"Dad, Dad!" Big Guy yelled as he jumped up into Devereaux's strong arms.

"How's my Big Guy doing today?" Devereaux asked as he hugged his boy.

"Me and Johnny were catching pollywogs down at Hartwell Park Pond!" Big Guy exclaimed.

"You don't have any of them in the backyard do you?" Devereaux inquired. "Your mom will have a fit if she finds them." He continued.

"No I left them at Johnny's house", Big Guy replied.

"Good- the Milner house is a good place to keep frogs", Devereaux replied with a smile.

About that moment Big Guy heard the distant whistle of the Helms Bakery Truck, or simply the "Donut Man" as he was known to all the kids in the neighborhood. Big Guy reached into his pocket and found the quarter that his Uncle Jim had given him last week. Uncle Jim was his mother's brother, and he always had a quarter for his nephews when he came to visit. Big Guy stood by the curb and gazed down the street waiting for the beige colored panel truck to appear. It had been several minutes since the last whistle had sounded and Big Guy was beginning to worry that the Donut Man had bypassed his street.

Then he was there, as if by magic, the whistle blew from down at the end of the street. As the shiny panel truck turned onto Big Guy's street, children and mothers appeared out of nowhere and crowded onto the curb in scattered groups up and down the tree- lined street. It seemed like an eternity before the shining truck approached Big Guy, who had been joined by Mrs. Wildman from next door. The truck stopped and a man in a tan uniform, complete with a police cap and a bow tie, jumped out of the cab and met Big Guy and Mrs. Wildman at the back of the truck. At the back of the truck was an awning that stuck out 4 feet from above the twin access doors that enclosed a series of large wooden drawers. As the driver opened the doors, the aroma of fresh hot bread and donuts filled the air. To Big Guy it was a solemn experience; as if the portal to heaven itself had been opened.

"What would you like ma'am?" asked the Donut Man to Mrs. Wildman.

"I would like a loaf of white bread and ten dinner rolls please", Mrs. Wildman replied.

Big Guy stared as the transaction took place. "Thank you", Mrs. Wildman replied as she walked back to her house.

"And how about you Sir?' the Donut Man asked Big Guy.

"Can I see your donuts?" Big Guy asked.

The Donut Man smiled and then pulled open the large drawer closest to the bottom. Big Guy's eyes widened as the drawer was pulled out. There, neatly stacked in rows were donuts of every description, including jelly filled, cream filled, glazed and frosted donuts. Donut twists, chocolate donuts and Danish pastries. Just then a light breeze carried the scent of jelly and sugar into Big Guy's face.

"What can I get for a quarter?" Big Guy asked. "You can get one jelly donut or two of these glazed donuts here", the Donut Man replied.

"I will take two of those glazed donuts", Big Guy replied with a smile. The Donut Man picked up the two donuts with a piece of wax paper and handed them to Big Guy.

Big Guy's hands shook as he grabbed the donuts and handed the Donut Man his quarter. "Thank you!" Big Guy replied. As the Donut

Man drove away, Big Guy's brother Brian wandered up with his friend John.

"What do you have there Gore?" Brian asked with a smile.

Big Guy sensed trouble and started to run as his brother Brian laughed and pretended to give chase.

"These are my donuts!" Big Guy yelled as he spared no time running away from his brother carrying one donut in his mouth. Just then Big Guy tripped on the edge of the sidewalk as the donut in his hand rolled into a nearby flower bed.

"See what you did!" Big Guy yelled back at his brother as he tried to hold back tears. Picking up the fallen donut, Big Guy inspected it. After removing a few twigs and dirt, Big Guy ate the donut and walked back home. As Big Guy walked into the house his mother said, "You better not let those donuts spoil your dinner."

"Donuts?" Big Guy replied with a spot of glazed sugar on his cheek.

Soon all six kids and their parents were seated around a large dining room table. And before the boys could start poking at one another, Priscilla began to pray as the rest joined in.

"Bless us oh Lord for these thy gifts for which we are about to receive through Christ our Lord, Amen"

Big Guy noted that the tempo of this sacred prayer seemed to increase rapidly toward its end as the Meehans prepared for the daily dinner battle in which a sea of hands reached simultaneously for whatever was served. At which point Priscilla turned into a referee and gatekeeper of food portions.

"One of you kids at a time!" Priscilla would exclaim as she dished up each plate, starting with Devereaux.

While none of the Meehan children ever went hungry, the competition at the dinner table was always keen. However vegetables like peas and carrots always seemed to be plentiful and not subject to as much attention as the main course. During Sunday dinner, especially when fried chicken was the main entree, the competition was especially keen between the oldest Meehan brothers Steve and Dan. Steve, knowing that he was limited by Priscilla on how many drumsticks that he could have, would turn to good old fashioned capitalism to procure more of his mother's tasty chicken.

In hushed tones Steve would turn to Dan and ask, "Hey Dan- I will give you fifty cents for your drumstick." To which Dan would answer, "Get your own drumstick!"

Each member of the Meehan Clan had their own unique relationship to the other. To Big Guy there was a special connection with his oldest brother Steve. When Devereaux wasn't around, Steve became Big Guy's surrogate father and protector. Big Guy's brother Brian was at times a protector and at other times an antagonist. Always the first to harass Big Guy at Christmas or Halloween by grabbing his presents or snatching his candy, Brian served to keep his little brother "in line".

Big Guy learned the importance of family trust the hard way; it was taught to him by the rest of his brothers one day when Big Guy had "Snitched" on his brother's party plans. They had planned a party one day when their parents were going to be away. Big Guy spilled the beans when he mentioned it to Priscilla one afternoon.

After learning that their party plans had been disclosed by their little brother, the Meehan boys figured that it was time to teach their youngest sibling a lesson about trust. A few days later Big Guy was walking down the long hallway leading to the boy's bedroom when Steve and Dan stepped out at the end of the hallway to block his path. Seeing this Big Guy turned to walk back toward the living room, only to be blocked by his brother Brian. Big

Guy knew that his day of reckoning had arrived.

"So you like to tell do you?" Steve hissed as the older Meehan boys closed in on their little brother. It was like a classic mafia hit from the movies. Only the "hit" wasn't carried out with deadly force, but with something that seemed more painful at the time.

Big Guy never did snitch on his brothers from that day forward. Not even when asked by his mother what had happened to his blackened eye?

Big Guy was certainly no saint back in the early days and his brother Brian was not the constant source of consternation that Big Guy considered him it be. At times Brian could be a guardian angel, like the day that Big Guy decided to play Tarzan on the venation blinds in the front room. After jumping off the back of the couch, the pull cord on the blinds slipped around Big Guy's neck, leaving him struggling to free himself as he swung from side to side. After his sister Sheila spotted her little brother swinging by his neck, she pointed it out to Brian who raced to free Big Guy from catastrophe. On another occasion Big Guy thought that it would be a good idea to roast marshmallows in the backyard next to the house. Just as the newspapers were flaming up toward the roof, Brian happened by and extinguished the small inferno before it caught the roof on fire. Then as if to add insult to injury Brian started to slowly walk away as he said with a smile, "I'm going to tell mom."

"No- don't tell mom!", Big Guy cried. Big Guy knew that once his mom knew then his dad would know too. "Please don't tell mom!" Big Guy pleaded desperately as his brother continued to walk toward the kitchen.

"I'm going to tell mom", Brian continued with a smile.

Big Guy resigned himself at that moment to his impending punishment. Fortunately it was his mother welding the belt that afternoon and not his father.

One day in March of 1966, Big Guy was lying on his back watching his kite glide ever higher toward the puffy spring clouds above him. A cool sea breeze was steadily blowing off the great Pacific, as Big Guy's mind wandered with the kite as it searched for the thermals which would lift it even higher. In his mind the world could not be more at peace, yet Big Guy's life was about to get sucked into the turbulence that defined the late 1960's. One can never quite define the point at which their life changes. But with Big Guy it started at that moment when a passing airplane on its approach to Long Beach Airport happened to snag the string to his kite as it passed overhead.

At about the time the Piper Cub passed by his kite, Big Guy noticed the kite suddenly get violently jerked in the direction that the airplane was flying. It was strange to feel the thrust of a passing airplane reverberating in his hands as the string inched along the rear wheel of the aircraft.

"Oh No!" Big Guy exclaimed, thinking that he would somehow cause the small plane to crash. Just then the string broke and his kite floated away. Big Guy watched the kite until it drifted several blocks away from the park. After some hard searching, Big Guy found his kite in an alley a mile away. It was a random event that somehow marked the start of the turbulent times ahead.

Chapter 2

The 1960's – The Wave Meets the Rock

The year was 1966 as the ground beneath their feet started to move. The American landscape started to shift as millions of people like the Meehan's came of age. Growing expectations that matched their growing level of affluence enveloped them during that time of hope and trepidation.

Every Southern California native knows that earthquakes start slowly with a rumble, then ring like a bell through a landscape that seems solid and unchanging. The shaken souls cling to the hope that their beliefs will sustain them through the turmoil that rapid change brings. Like the foundation of Devereaux's childhood home in the aftermath of the 1933 Long Beach Earthquake, Devereaux's beliefs where shaken to their foundation by what was about to befall his family in the late 1960's.

In early September of 1966, Priscilla's mother passed away as Priscilla helplessly watched. Priscilla had left the convent, yet her deep faith had never left her. Priscilla always had a way of looking at the world that was timeless and unique. She was a wise woman who studied the fine lines of meaning between what people said and what they were thinking. In the final moments of her mother's fading life, Priscilla had noticed a brilliant blue come into her mother's eyes as she left this life. It was a sign to Priscilla that her mother had been at peace when she passed. In spite of the peace of her passing, her mother's death had been a trying time for Priscilla. Perhaps it was the growing rebellion of her oldest children, or the uncertainty of her son Larry's latest medical tests that worried Priscilla the most.

Larry was the closest to Big Guy in age and the two brothers always seemed to have an intense competition going on with each other. Where Larry was, there too was Big Guy not very far away. Larry was a creative and curious little boy, always taking things apart to see how they worked. Larry watched in awe as astronauts on TV would walk in space as he swore that he would one day work for NASA. While Big Guy was aggressive and outgoing, Larry was passive and introspective. The two were quite the contrast to each other as both would race to Devereaux's lap in the evening, only to poke at each other from behind their father's head.

Larry was eleven years old in 1966 and he seemed to always be tired and run down. Something was not right with Larry and Priscilla knew it. It was not long before the medical tests revealed that Devereaux and Priscilla's fifth child was dying from a rare and deadly form of cancer known as Neuroblastoma, which results in malignant tumors that develop from within nerve tissue.

Soon Priscilla was busy taking Larry to the hospital for his chemotherapy, between operations aimed at removing the numerous tumors that were growing within his deteriorating young body. When he returned home, a now thin and balding shell of his former self, Larry would show off his long scars like badges of courage as the hearts of his family slowly broke. Larry's long suffering continued until August of 1967, when he died in Priscilla's arms just a week before his twelfth birthday. In the final moments of Larry's life, with the cancer invading his lungs leaving him struggling to breath, he looked in fear to his mother as she told him to ask for God's help in finding his breath. After the third plea to God, Larry died.

Big Guy was almost nine years old and he did not fully understand the meaning of this turmoil. On the night of his brother's death Big Guy looked to Devereaux for comfort. After some searching, Big Guy finally found him, sitting alone on the front porch in the dark, with tears streaming down his face.

Shrouded in a profound sadness Devereaux stoically faced his family and his relationship to it. It was then that Big Guy learned that the world was not as solid and unchanging as he had come to believe. Big Guy embraced his father as Devereaux struggled to compose himself. Big Guy had never seen his father cry before, as his father had always towered like a rock in his mind.

"Sometimes you just can't win for losing," Devereaux said.

"Mom says that Larry's in a better place," Big Guy replied as if to reassure his father.

"He's our little Saint in heaven," Devereaux replied.

"Why does God allow people to die?" Big Guy asked his father.

"I wish I knew Big Guy." Devereaux replied as he stared at the stars above them.

Priscilla and Devereaux struggled to find some sense of reason, some piece of wreckage to cling to and yet the waves kept coming, as the Meehan siblings started to rebel.

First, it was against their Catholic upbringing, in which they abandoned the same Catholic high school that their parents once attended. Instead, they insisted on attending the nearby public school, which Devereaux referred to as "Toilet Tech." Then it was what they chose to wear and who they had as friends.

The question of race, as with all Americans, was a complex mix of good and bad in Devereaux's life. While he had been raised Catholic in a generally Hispanic part of the nation like his mother had, Devereaux had grown up in a bigoted world, where minorities had been marginalized. To Devereaux the world had a social order, where everyone knew their place and only hard work could ever liberate those born into it. The interesting part of this equation was that Devereaux's mother Ethel had been looked down upon by her nativist in laws for being Irish and Catholic.

One day Devereaux answered the door only to find a multiracial group of young people standing on his front porch. A young Hispanic man asked Devereaux, "Excuse us Mr. Meehan, but is Sheila available?"

A startled Devereaux walked back into the house and shouted, "Hey Sheila, the League of Nations is looking for you on the front porch."

His own children now questioned the narrow stereotypes that made Devereaux's world comfortable. As the world grew more complex, so did the challenges to all that Devereaux held dear.

The Meehan kids had long ago embraced rock and roll music, which irked their father

every time he heard it. To Devereaux, Rock
and Roll was just a symptom of something
deeper that was threatening to weaken the
fabric of America. Once in a fit of rage
Devereaux broke several of Big Guy's older
brothers' Beatles albums. Devereaux was not
going to stand for "that Limey Crap" in his
house. It was not as if such behavior was
unheard of in the Meehan house. Only a few
weeks before this incident the two oldest
Meehan's, Steve and Dan were attending the
guitar lessons that Priscilla had arranged for
them. They were in their bedroom practicing
when an altercation erupted between them.
Before they knew it, both guitars had been
broke over each other's heads. To the Meehan
boys, it had all been so much for the notion of
culture among barbarians.

Big Guy had always noticed that Devereaux
had a prejudice against the British, and it was
difficult for him to understand why; until one
day he listened to his grandmother Ethel speak
negatively of the British. Being the child of
Irish Immigrants Ethel carried the same
resentment as her parents, who had suffered
starvation and discrimination at the hands of
the British during the Great Famine. After
more than a century, hatred was hard to let go
of within the hearts of the hungry.

Like most children of the baby boom generation, Big Guy's older siblings were caught up in the change and looking to experiment with the next possibility. To Priscilla and Devereaux it was like trying to herd ants. The more they tried to control their children, the more those children would try their parents. In addition to rock and roll, sex and drugs occupied Big Guy's older siblings during those turbulent years.

One evening while Priscilla and Devereaux were out to dinner at a nice restaurant, the Meehan Boys decided that it would be a good time to have a party. As the home brew flowed and more teenagers showed up at the door, Big Guy began to understand that nothing good could become of the situation. Soon the house was alive with laughter and carousing. Big Guy's brothers were members of a local club called the "Serfs". Now the Serfs were mostly harmless teenagers looking for a good time and were seldom associated with any real mischief. On this night, the club was to perform several initiation ceremonies, which included a great deal of drinking, followed by the obligatory spanking of new inductees with a two by four board.

All had a good time up until someone noticed headlights pulling up into the driveway. It was Devereaux and Priscilla.

The rush was on! Big Guy watched teenagers flee the house in all directions. Everyone understood that Devereaux had a terrible temper and no one wanted to be around when he lost his temper.

Through the back door they ran and over the back fence they jumped, some of them tripping from the effects of too much alcohol. Big Guy's brothers scrambled to straighten up the house as one of their friends took refuge in the bushes by the driveway. He was discovered as a pair of legs under a rose bush in the headlights of Devereaux's car.

After Devereaux parked the car in the garage, he walked into the house to the smell of cigarette smoke and a few scattered beer bottles.

"What in the hell has been going on here?" Devereaux bellowed.

To which Big Guy's brother Dan replied, "Nothing Dad we just had a few friends over."

"You better get your asses into gear and clean this place up." Devereaux shouted.

As he looked over his shoulder into the driveway, Devereaux noticed one of Dan's friends running down the driveway as if the hounds of hell were after him. To Devereaux it was just another example of his children led astray by the perils of modern life. He was afraid that it would not be the last time and he was right.

As the oldest brothers tangled with the law and his sister overdosed on sleeping pills, a strangely wonderful and unexpected individual came into Big Guy's life. He was a kid only a few years older than Big Guy. He had moved into the neighborhood brandishing a butterfly net and field guides to identify insects and birds. As Big Guy soon learned, this newcomer was a "slow" kid, and he soon became the bravest outcast Big Guy had ever met. With his newfound inspiration, Big Guy started to occupy himself by collecting bugs and studying the natural world around him. Upon first glance, the natural world was hard to find in Southern California. After some years, in contrast to the mayhem of 1960s Los Angeles, the natural world became Big Guy's "road less taken". It became the revelation that ultimately saved Big Guy from the chaos that swirled around him during those turbulent days.

As 1967 rolled into 1968, the streets of Southern California soon teemed with strange looking people from all across the nation. "Road Lice", Devereaux would remark as he drove by the small groups of Hippies hitchhiking along the Pacific Coast Highway. They were indeed "different", but some of the girls were still attractive to Big Guy as he was now starting to take notice of such things. Much to Devereaux's chagrin, Sheila was soon bringing home long haired boyfriends. They were not "the one" to Sheila. There was only one true boyfriend and he was a Marine, patrolling the jungle somewhere around DaNang, in South Vietnam in 1968. Occasionally Big Guy received letters from Sheila's Marine. Big Guy appreciated the Marine's thoughtfulness and he would reply with encouragement. But that war soon destroyed any hope that may have survived in the Marine. When Sheila's Marine came home in late 1969, he was a changed man. Like so many who had served in Vietnam, he returned haunted and detached from who he was when he had left. By the fall of 1969, much about America had become detached.

As Priscilla struggled to deal with the deaths of her mother and her son, she found comfort in the emerging voices taking shape on the national scene in America during those troubled times. Among the voices that gave Priscilla hope were Martin Luther King Jr. and Robert Kennedy. To Priscilla they represented the peaceful revolution that Christ Himself had brought to the world. But we all know what happened to Christ for speaking the truth.

It was a spring day in April of 1968 when Priscilla heard the news of the assassination of

Martin Luther King Jr. in Memphis. She spent the night in tears as the fresh scars of loss reopened. This great granddaughter of southern slaveholders had lost a sense of redemption in the person of the great civil rights leader, whom she characterized as a "great bearer of Christ's teachings."

On the next night, Devereaux and Big Guy went to fetch Grandma Ethel from her home in downtown Long Beach. As they headed toward the downtown section of the city, Big Guy noticed the black columns of smoke rising from toward Los Angeles. Watts was burning and the riots were starting to spread. Devereaux wanted to ensure that his mother was going to be safe so he had decided to bring grandma to stay with the family for a while. As they neared the inner city, it was surreal to see armed troops with fixed bayonets occupying street corners.

America's avoidance of any discussion of the subject of race had once again incited trouble. Big Guy did not fully understand the implications of what he saw that day, but it had something to do with the attitude that his father revealed whenever the subject of race was discussed. Big Guy would not say that Devereaux was a racist, but he was indeed a bigot.

Like Priscilla's family', the Meehan's had originally come from the South. Two hundred years after leaving the South, old views of the world died hard in the Meehan family. Sadly, the use of the word "Nigger" was not rare in the family. Devereaux viewed most minorities with the stereotype that was common among the many generations of the working class.

Strangely enough, Devereaux was just as prejudiced against white southerners as he was blacks. Later in life, the race issue was the closest Big Guy ever came to challenging Devereaux directly. While only viewing racism from his own detached perspective, it was Big Guy himself, who experienced the rage that racism represented within his society and his own family.

Like the effect that Grandma Ethel's parents had on her, Big Guy found that he was himself caught in the same generational trap of prejudice and fear. He was forced to confront that legacy one day in the spring, when Big Guy walked over to Wardlow Park and discovered that a large church group of African Americans were having a picnic in the park. It was surprising to Big Guy to see so many black people. He had never been around African Americans before and had only known them by the disparaging remarks of his brothers and his father over the years. Big Guy watched as children played the same games that he played on any given day at this park. To Big Guy the park seemed different that day; it had an atmosphere that seemed more tense and uncertain.

Big Guy walked into the game room and looked to see if any of his friends were around. Before long he found his friend Johnny, who was sitting on a bench watching the kids playing board games. Big Guy walked over towards John, when one of the African American kid's named Jonathan confronted Big Guy. Jonathan was not a very large kid, but he was a cocky kid, just like Big Guy.

"Sit down". Jonathan said in a low tone as he stared at Big Guy.

At first Big Guy did not understand what Jonathan was saying. Big Guy asked him to repeat the question. While he could not understand the question, Big Guy could see that Jonathan was getting agitated as he once again told him to "Sit down".

Big Guy answered, "I'm just passing by to see my friend over there".

Once again, Jonathan approached Big Guy and commanded him to "Sit down".

It was an example of two people not understanding anything about one another. Big Guy could hardly understand Jonathan's speech; its cadence and accent. Jonathan was obviously feeling that Big Guy had invaded his space. To Big Guy the nature of the encounter was a mystery. One thing that wasn't a mystery was the national context in which this exchange was occurring. There was no real dialog, only frustration and an underlying rage.

By this time, Big Guy did not appreciate the attitude of this newcomer to the park, and being that Big Guy was a member of the local Meehan Clan; he did not see any reason to back down from this escalating situation. Big Guy looked at Jonathan and replied, "No I don't think I have to sit down, I'm just passing by."

Upon hearing this, Jonathan shoved Big Guy toward a nearby bench. Instantly Big Guy grabbed Jonathan in a headlock and drove him to the ground. As the two wrestled with each other, a crowd of both black and white kids encircled the fight and began shouting calls of support to each opponent. As Big Guy proceeded to choke Jonathan, Jonathan started to scratch Big Guy's face with his finger nails. Within the context of race and a summer of rioting, Big Guy came face to face with the dark side of himself and the society within which he had grown up. Soon one of the park attendants pulled the two enraged combatants apart. Big Guy began to curse as tears of rage rolled down his face.

Big Guy shouted at the assembled crowd of African Americans in the terminology of rage,

"You dirty niggers!" he shouted with all the spite in his heart.

At first, there was silence, as if those black kids had never heard that epitaph from an actual white person before. To Big Guy it was as if those words had come from someone else's mouth.

The African American children finally shouted back, "You white paddy!"

Big Guy had not heard the term "White Paddy" before and he found himself struck by the notion that people would characterize him in such a manner. The park attendant finally pulled the two away from each other and continued to break up the group of children, sending them away from the game room.

Some of the African American children shouted, "We're going to riot you!"

Later that day Big Guy and Johnny were riding bicycles through the park, when they passed by an old shed and while Johnny kept on riding, Big Guy suddenly found himself surrounded by about fifty angry African American kids. They had remembered him from the incident earlier in the day and were now out for their revenge. Words could not describe the look on his friend Johnny's face as the angry mob enveloped Big Guy. It was a look of complete helplessness as Big Guy looked back at Johnny and nodded his head, as if to give his friend permission to abandon him to his fate. It was a situation that had played out many times over the course of history; only this time it was not a lynch mob of angry white racists and a solitary black victim.

After some small talk, the beating began and it took all the strength that Big Guy possessed to break free from the swinging fists. At some point, his attackers were distracted and Big Guy took the opportunity to escape. He was fortunate to escape with only two black eyes and several bruises on his arms and back.

Over the years, Big Guy came to gain a better empathy for people. To Big Guy, everyone was a product of their past and the context in which they were raised. That was not an excuse for racism; it was merely a fact of life. Discrimination served only to degrade everyone. He never held a grudge against African Americans, but he had become aware of just how deep racism went in his society and that it existed in all people to some extent. Big Guy had learned that racism not only got in the way of progress and a better society for everyone, it created division that threatened the nation's very existence. Devereaux had no such revelations at that point in time.

There was an excitement in the air in late May of 1968. Big Guy did not have a clue about what was happening in the larger world around him, but his parents were constantly chatting about the upcoming presidential election. Big Guy's oldest brothers were concerned about the draft for the war in Vietnam. A young man from the neighborhood was killed in Vietnam a year earlier, and it reminded all that the war was more than violent images on the evening news.

Big Guy remembered when that same young man had earlier saved his life after he had fallen in a swimming pool. Just as the water started to fill his lungs, Big Guy remembered those strong arms pulling him toward the light. He was the same young man who had volunteered to help medevac other dying souls who had also been grasping toward the light, only to fall to earth with the two pilots in the shell of a battered helicopter.

Both sides of the Meehan family had been Democrats since before the Civil War. Progressive Populism formed the bedrock of their political beliefs and as the election of Robert F. Kennedy became a distinct possibility; Big Guy's parents became hopeful that the America that they had known was still alive and well.

Big Guy had gotten a hold of a handful of Kennedy for President bumper stickers and was by that time busy pasting them over every Nixon poster that he could find. Big Guy felt a sense of a rising hope within his family, if not the nation as a whole. One day in June Big Guy came home to find his mother crying in despair. "*Robert F. Kennedy shot to death in Los Angeles*" was the headline on the television in front of her. The hope that Priscilla had known seemed to die with the second Kennedy. She had lost so much, in such a rapid succession. What could she ever do to recover what had been lost? What could any of the Meehan's do to recover the remnants of their family?

Chapter 3

The First Trip North

In Southern California during the 1960s, people were defined by what kind of vehicle they drove. Surfers drove jacked up cars with surfboard racks, Hot Rodders drove modified race cars, rich College Kids drove sports cars, Mexicans drove low riders and Bikers rode Harleys. Big Guy's brothers drove low riders, complete with custom wheels, tuck and roll upholstery and Glaspack Mufflers. Perhaps they were confused Catholics, or maybe just enough of the old Southern California had rubbed off on them over the years that they were Chicanos at heart.

Whatever the reason the Meehan boys had no problem finding other low riders to hang around with in the neighborhood. On any given day one could find them sitting in large circles with the other neighborhood hoodlums on the grass at Wardlow Park. There they would carouse, while smoking cigarettes and talking about whatever the latest neighborhood gossip happened to be. During these informal meetings Big Guy would wander over to harass his brothers and "hang with the guys".

"Are you taking Jeanie Carson out this Saturday?" Joe Alvarado asked Big Guy's brother Dan.

"No, Rod and I are going to a party over on Stanbridge this Saturday, I hear that there will be lots of girls there", Dan replied.

Just then Steve, the oldest of the Meehan boys showed up with two of his friends.

"What are you turds up to?" Steve asked as he sat down on the grass next to Dan, where he promptly wiped his nose on the back of Dan's t-shirt.

"Steve-you are an asshole!" Dan exclaimed as he pushed his older brother away.

"We're trying to figure out what is going on this weekend", Joe replied.

"You still have problems with the carb on your car?" Steve asked.

"Ya- it is a piece of shit!" Joe exclaimed. "I have rebuilt it twice and still no go."

"You're not going to get laid without a car Joe", Steve said with a smile.

"Speaking of getting laid, did you hear that Ben Watson is going out with Amanda Greer?" Dave Kern said with a smile.

"No way!" Rod Bergman replied.

Just then Bill Peck walked up to the group and interrupted, "Hey did you guys hear what happened to Jimmy Rodriguez?!"

"He was blown away man!" Bill repeated to himself as if in shock, "Blown away!"

"He just left three weeks ago!" Dan Meehan replied.

"It seemed like he was just out of boot camp yesterday man", Joe said.

"Oh shit, his sister Gina…..she has got to be hurtin", Joe continued.

A long silence followed, as the group stared at the grass or off into space. Vietnam had once again interjected itself into the lives of the kids in the Meehan's neighborhood. The draft was beginning to impact the oldest of that generation, especially for those who were not able to attend school. To some it was like a death sentence and to others it was an abstract adventure, just like the John Wayne movies that they had grown up with.

Big Guy was trying hard to "blend in" hoping that his big brothers would forget that he was there. But it wasn't long before they spotted him and chased him off with dirt clods and threats. Big Guy heard many things while sitting in those daily "talking circles". Big Guy had a front row seat to the perceptions of those young people growing up in a rapidly changing America, where questions of love and war intersected with the longing of a whole generation. Those discussions served to enlarge Big Guy's perception of the world around him back in those tumultuous days.

As Devereaux would say, "There was a little bit of Oklahoma" in the Meehan family. Meaning that there was an unorthodox streak and a tendency to improvise that ran though the family. That statement rang especially true when Big Guy's oldest brother Steve was driving an old Studebaker that regularly burned and leaked oil. At this time Devereaux was working on the offshore oil production facilities that dotted the coast of Southern California. It was just a year before Union Oil's Platform A blew out in the Santa Barbara Channel in 1969 and Devereaux was working lots of overtime. It was at this time that Devereaux was regularly providing Steve with jugs of crude oil to dump into the old Studebaker. Devereaux figured that the Rockefellers' would never miss a few quarts of crude. He would remind Steve that all he had to do was "Change the oil filter more often". Before the engine finally blew up, Big Guy watched as old Steve blasted off down the street in a blue cloud of victory. To the Meehan's, it was a victory over the industrial titans of the age and proved that some days belonged to the little people.

One day Big Guy came home to find his brother Brian tinkering with two speakers out of an old car. Big Guy watched as Brian soon fabricated a wire mount from a clothes hanger that allowed the car speakers to be placed on one's head like headphones. After this Brian attached two speaker wires into the family stereo, Big Guy watched as Brian powered up side one of Jimi Hendrix's "*Experience*". Brian smiled as the vinyl record rotated to the start of "*Purple Haze*".

"Can I try them on?" Big Guy asked as Brian passed the home made headphones to his little brother. Big Guy placed the bulky headphones over his ears as his brother adjusted the volume.

"Wow!" Big Guy exclaimed, "The sound is traveling through my head!" As the sound of stereo alternated from one speaker to the other, Big Guy bobbed back and forth to the beat, like a buoy in the ocean. Brian removed the speakers from Big Guy's head as Big Guy started to play an imaginary "air guitar" as he walked from the room.

Southern California was the home of Hollywood and was regarded as the Madison Avenue of the West. Big Guy grew up a mere twenty miles from the media capital of the world and its influence was everywhere. He had spent his life watching commercials on TV, to the point that his family would chide him for remembering every slogan and jingle long after he had seen it. One afternoon Big Guy went to the local Market Basket with Priscilla and discovered the Oscar Meyer Weanermobile parked in the parking lot.

"Look mom there it is!" Big Guy exclaimed. "The Weanermobile!" The Weanermobile was a large red fiberglass hotdog on a yellow bun shaped chassis with wheels. Around the middle of the hot dog was the Oscar Meyer label. Big Guy ran over to the Weanermobile and marveled at it until his mother finally coaxed him away from the unusual vehicle. As they entered the supermarket, Big Guy spotted Little Oscar, the official Oscar Meyer spokesperson handing out plastic whistles shaped like little weaners. Before long Big Guy had his and was joining the shrill of shrieking weaner whistles that filled the grocery store. Such was life in the 1960s, where advertising became blurred with reality to form a confusing noise which eventually challenged our faith in everything that we thought that we knew to be real.

One night in the spring of 1968 Devereaux was scanning the classified ads in the Press-Telegram, when he came across an ad for 4 acres of land in North Central Washington State. He asked if Big Guy wanted to go with him to see about the land. Big Guy agreed and they jumped into Devereaux's green VW Bug and drove toward North Long Beach. The transaction was an interesting encounter in itself. The land was offered by a merchant sailor who had won it in a card game. Big Guy would never forget the sailor, who was an older man, who had grey hair and a tattoo on his left arm of a green mermaid with the initials L.D. above the figure. After Devereaux shook hands with him, he proceeded to describe the land in detail.

"I was in the Philippine Sea off Mindanao and the cook and I were having one a hell of a card game. He says to me as he laid his cards down, "Beat this Sonny." He laid down a Three of Clubs and two pairs-Kings and Jacks as I remember. To which I replied, "Contemplate this Bub", as I dazzled him with a full house. It was a sweet victory and he pulled out the deed from his sea-chest and told me that we would square things up when we got to Seattle. He was good to his word and here we are."

The sailor gazed out into space, his mind thousands of miles away on the rolling waves of the Pacific.

"It's kind of remote", the sailor said. "It took me awhile to find it."

"The last time I was in those parts of the world the Japs were sinking ships in the neighborhood. You can have that part of the world," Devereaux said with a smile.

"Is there power nearby?" Devereaux asked.

"Not hardly", the sailor replied with a smile.

"You best have a generator."

"Can you grow anything on it? How about water- does it have any water on it?" Devereaux asked.

"I heard that someone once tried to grow mushrooms on it. There's a well there that overflows in the spring. It's nothing special-just a piece of raw ground," the sailor replied.

It was a purchase that would change Big Guy's life forever. On the way home, Devereaux turned into the Cal Store gas station to top off his tank. Cal Store was having a "Gas War" at the time with a service station across the street. It would be a unique day in Big Guy's life; not only for the fact that regular gasoline was 19 cents per gallon, a price that he would never see again in his life, but Devereaux purchased four acres of undeveloped land in North Central Washington State for $250.00 cash.

One day in late April of 1968 Big Guy found Devereaux loading up the Volkswagen Bug that he had bought brand new the year before.

Big Guy asked, "Where are you going Dad?"

To this Devereaux replied, "God's country". Then he looked at Big Guy with a smile and asked, "No one else wants to -so how would you like to come with me Big Guy?"

"Can I- what about school?" Big Guy replied with excitement.

"Go ask your mom", Devereaux said.

As Big Guy ran to ask his mother, she seemed to already know his question, "Yes you can go with your Dad, just be careful", his mom said with a smile.

"Wow I get to travel with dad and play hooky from school!" thought Big Guy as he rushed to pack his clothes.

They soon had everything stuffed into the back seat of the little VW. Devereaux and Big Guy gave Priscilla a hug as she gave them her traditional mom blessing, "May God bless and keep you and bring you home safe to me please."

Off they went in a VW Bug that was stuffed to the brim with an ice chest, camping gear and clothes, toward a destination that would forever influence their lives in ways they could never imagine.

Devereaux and Big Guy headed north on Interstate 405; as Big Guy watched the congestion of the city pass by he thought about what "God's Country" was like. "What's it like up there Dad?" he asked.

"It's green and pretty", Devereaux replied as a Ford LTD lurched in front of him.

"Piss Ant!" Devereaux exclaimed as he slammed on the breaks. "There's a man that needs a forty eight hour enema in his left ear", Devereaux said as he swerved to avoid the intrusion. Soon the LTD pulled across several more lanes of traffic and sped away in the mass of traffic that hurled itself north along the freeway. "That's right fella; hurry on back to Des Moines, your mother is calling."

Devereaux always had colorful ways of exhibiting his frustrations, and somehow his children always understood the hidden meaning, which Devereaux seemed to weave into every discussion.

After Devereaux's temper improved, he settled back into the subject of what Big Guy could expect when they got to "God's Country". "You will love it up there", Devereaux said with a smile.

It was then that Big Guy remembered all the evenings in which Devereaux and he would sit on the front porch, looking at the night sky while Devereaux spoke of the "North Woods" and "Wenatchee".

Devereaux spoke of these places as though he was speaking of heaven itself. After the death of Larry and all that the family had been through, it was a blessing to think that any sense of heaven could exist in the wreckage of those times. Big Guy did not know where Wenatchee was, but it must have been a beautiful place.

It was strange to consider that Big Guy's grandparents from both sides of the family had come to Southern California in the first decade of the 20th century, to escape rural lives in which stormy weather and personal struggle had formed their sense of success.

To Devereaux's father Frank, Southern California must have been heaven. Frank had moved from Eastern Oregon to find a better life in a sunny place where there was opportunity and room to grow. Heaven it seems adapts itself to the dreams of those who seek it. Two generations later Big Guy was looking to return to those stormy places up north, where one could appreciate the beauty of bad weather and search for some missing connection in which to anchor his turbulent life.

There they were, stuck in Southern California traffic within a sea of humanity; trapped in a world of confusion surrounded by the ticky tacky that was the contemporary American Dream of the 1960s. They might not have fully understood it at the time but Devereaux and Big Guy were both longing for a different existence, in a simpler world free from the turmoil of "progress" and the aftermath of failed expectations. Big Guy's mind and spirit had already left Southern California for dead. Big Guy must not have been alone in this thought, for within a decade the demographics of Los Angeles County would reflect a mass migration out of the area.

Soon the city gave way to the native vegetation of Southern California; graceful Live Oaks and Manzanita covered the grassy slopes of the Grapevine as the underpowered VW struggled to carry its heavy burden over the hump toward Bakersfield.

"What is an Okie Baby's third word Piggies?" Devereaux asked.

"I don't know Dad, what is it?" Big Guy replied, curious to learn something new about the world around him.

"It's Mama, Papa, and Bakersfield", Devereaux replied with a laugh, thoroughly entertained by his own joke.

His laughter turned somber as Devereaux spoke of watching the Dust Bowl migration that he witnessed as a child growing up in Southern California during the Great Depression. He described the old dusty cars and trucks from Oklahoma and Texas that hauled the gaunt faces of battered lives through his own quiet home town; so far removed from the thick clouds of swirling soil and the hot dry winds that destroyed the lives of so many. He told of all their possessions attached to their vehicles as they drove through town on their way to the San Joaquin Valley to start their lives anew. They were refugees like those from a war zone. That war zone had been the United States of the 1930's and Devereaux's native California had become their promised land.

As he spoke Devereaux's face seemed to search inward as if to make sense of what he had seen as a child. He then related the story of one individual who had remained in his memory more than all the others whose lives had passed within reach of his own during those desperate days. Devereaux told of a middle aged man who he had seen sitting on a park bench one day. The man held his head in his hands and seemed to be on his last shred of hope. His worn clothes revealed the past life of man who was once well off, living an average American life like everyone else. Yet here was the epitome of every American at this point of the Depression, one step away from total despair. It's one thing for a human being to be hungry, it is quite another for a human being to be in complete hopelessness and despair. Devereaux was haunted by this scene of personal calamity, as he continued to see that gaunt figure in his mind as he drove.

"I asked my dad if we could help the man in some way," Devereaux said sadly. "At first he resisted, but soon dad gave in and we went back to the park where we found the broken man still sitting on the park bench. Dad sized up the man to see if he was sober; he was very sober and hungry too. We escorted the gentleman to a nearby diner and bought him dinner; we had never seen someone so hungry. Come to find out the hungry man had once owned a small shoe business back in Chicago. After the crash there was no more business, not that folks stopped needing shoes, they just had other priorities. When the man finished his coffee, he thanked dad and disappeared into the crowds down on Pine Ave."

It was a stark vision that Big Guy could only imagine, however it seemed to live once again in the memory of Devereaux as they drove through Bakersfield on Highway 99 while on our migration to "God's Country" and our own promised land.

In a rest area north of Sacramento Devereaux and Big Guy spent the night only slightly tipped back in the front seats of the cramped VW Bug. In spite of the tight accommodations, they both managed to sleep just fine. The sun rose the next morning in a brilliant pink burst on the eastern horizon as Devereaux had a cup of coffee from a thermos behind the seat; Big Guy wandered to the edge of the rest area to get a view of the farm land that stretched for miles. Red Winged Blackbirds chased each other in the nearby cattails, as a solitary Marsh Hawk soared overhead. The smell of rich earth wafted through the cool morning air, as Big Guy's senses tuned into the new world that unfolded around him. To a city kid, these experiences were rare and exquisite. Each one changing his life incrementally, in unexpected ways and setting the stage for the path that he was to follow in his life.

After Devereaux finished his cup of coffee and checked the oil on the VW, they continued north on Highway 99 until they came to a roadside diner called the Olive Inn. Devereaux and Big Guy walked into the diner to a multitude of stares from the locals who gathered for their morning get together. The waitress, who was dressed in a pink striped dress with a white apron, approached them and asked if they wanted to sit at the counter or in a booth.

"A booth would be keen", said Devereaux as they followed the waitress to a booth facing the highway.

"Coffee honey?" asked the waitress as she turned the coffee cup that was sitting on the table up right.

"Sounds great!" said Devereaux as he and Big Guy settled into the booth.

"Well what do you think Big Guy?" Devereaux asked after the waitress filled his coffee cup.

"This is great!" Big Guy replied as he sensed the unique moment of sharing time with the real man who was his father.

"How long before we get to God's Country?" Big Guy asked.

"Should be there by tomorrow", Devereaux replied.

Big Guy then asked, " When did you first go there Dad?"

Devereaux paused and then looked out the window at the passing trucks on the highway and said, "During the war I was sent to the South Pacific on the mighty Ajax. I spent almost four years on a fleet repair ship. Me and 3,500 other misfits, he continued thoughtfully. We could repair anything- the ol Jax could. From torpedoes to whole ships, they called us to fix all kinds of stuff. It was better than having a damaged ship limp into some faraway port. At the end of the war they put us on a captured German ship called the *Day Star*, and we sailed from the Philippines to Seattle. We had been fighting the Japs and dysentery for over three years and we thought that we would never get back home. It took about three weeks or so to get there. Seattle was the first city that we came back to in our homeland after being gone for so long. It was like coming back to heaven itself."

Devereaux's eyes started to get misty as they scanned the old memories in his head. "When we pulled up to the dock there were high school bands playing and a lot of people cheering us and waving flags. The sun was out, but we were all cold from being in the tropics for so long. People were so nice there, they made us feel welcome".

After a moment of silence Devereaux continued, "Soon they sent me back to California, where I was discharged. It was nice to see my family again. Moving back to Seattle to look for work I discovered that the problem in Seattle, like most places after the war, was that there was housing shortages and this made it difficult to find a place to live. So I rented a room from the Crenitis Family and continued my electrical apprenticeship."

The server soon returned with the menus and refilled Devereaux's coffee cup. Devereaux continued, "Liberty Crenitis was a great lady, she treated me like a son. The Crenitis Family lived in a nice house on Woodlawn Avenue in Seattle. One thing that I loved about Seattle was the fact that there were no screens on the windows, and I never noticed any bugs. One morning I woke up and there was a robin standing on my bed post. It was amazing to see this bird in the house. When I woke up I startled the bird and it flew out the window. At breakfast, I mentioned this to Liberty and she became concerned that perhaps something was wrong at home. I think that the Greeks must have a superstition about birds in the house. She insisted that I call home and make sure that everyone was OK."

Soon the server returned and took their order. Devereaux continued, "I met some really swell people in Seattle when I lived there. I even met a really nice Lutheran girl."

"You had a girlfriend in Seattle?" Big Guy asked with surprise.

"It was before I met your mother." Devereaux quickly replied, "I went with her for about six months; she was a really sweet girl. But my mom, your grandmother Lefty, didn't think too highly of me getting involved with a girl who wasn't Catholic." Devereaux looked back to the highway.

"Just think Piggies, you might not be here if I had married that Lutheran girl."

"Yep, I guess I wouldn't be", Big Guy replied.

After breakfast they wandered back to the cramped VW and continued their journey north on Highway 99. By noon, the temperature hovered around 95° as they were approaching Red Bluff. As they traveled north, the flat rice fields of the Sacramento Valley gave way to the scattered oaks and rolling hills of Shasta County.

Soon they stopped at a Safeway in Redding to fill the ice chest with more ice and purchase lunch making supplies including baloney, cheese, crackers, buttermilk and 1/2 case of Lucky Lager. This was Devereaux's idea of good eating. After stopping at a gas station to fill up the VW and clean the windshield, they were on their way once again.

As they drove north, the landscape continued to transition from rolling hills and scattered oaks to brush and pine trees. Soon they came to Lake Shasta, which marked the completion of Interstate 5 through the Klamath Mountains. There spanning the lake, was a new high bridge that crossed one of its bays. Just as they had reached the crest of the bridge where the underpowered VW strained to maintain 50 miles per hour, a large truck came rumbling past with a large gust of air.

"Gott im Himmel!" Devereaux exclaimed as the little VW was pushed to the edge of the bridge by the rush of the passing truck.

Devereaux swerved to gain control once again.

It was the only German phrase Devereaux ever said. "God in Heaven" was Devereaux's way of taking the Lord's name in vain in a respectable fashion. Devereaux had an interesting way of cussing and while he had spent his whole life working in construction, where colorful language was a part of the culture, the "F word" was rarely a part of his lexicon.

They reached the Oregon border as the day started to wane. The little VW climbed higher into the Siskiyou Mountains as Big Guy's eyes grew heavy and he fell asleep. It was the next morning when he raised his head and looked around. They were in a field of daisies somewhere over the border in Washington State. Fog stretched out over a green, grassy landscape making for an ethereal scene of trees and wildflower filled meadows.

Devereaux slept in his seat, as Big Guy excitedly opened the door, and stepped out into this new world. From somewhere on the breeze came the smell of wood chips and burning cedar, while moisture from the Pacific Ocean to the west embraced the Douglas fir and hemlock forest that surrounded them on all sides.

As Big Guy stared out into the forest, a chipmunk scampered past. A Steller's jay flew from branch to branch in a nearby tree. Big

Guy saw plants that he had never before seen. Thimble berries, Alder and large Western Hemlock, new things that filled his young mind with wonder. The geography of one's life serves to provide a reference point in which to gage life's progress. The sights, smells and sounds of this new world stirred a deep wonder in him as it had Lewis and Clark, Magellan and Muir.

Soon Devereaux awoke and said, "We're getting close Aardvark."

Big Guy asked, "Where are we at Dad?"

Devereaux answered, "Around Centralia. We will be in Seattle in a few hours. How does fish sound for dinner?"

Big Guy had always loved seafood. He answered, "Fish sounds great! Where are we going to get some fish?" he continued, "Are we in Washington?"

To which Devereaux replied, "Yes Big Guy you have finally made it to Humptulips."

To Devereaux all of Washington State was "Humptulips".

"We are going to Ivars, that's where you get fish in Seattle", Devereaux continued.

At this time, a log truck rumbled by and being that they were parked near the haul road, they were engulfed in a cloud of dust. Big Guy thought that it was interesting how there could be dust with so much moisture in the air.

However, that was the nature of this new place. It was only two days ago that they had left Southern California, and now they were here in a field full of daisies being passed by a log truck.

Big Guy was splashing water on his face from the ice chest as Devereaux stepped out from behind a tree and proclaimed,

"I feel like I just lost 10 pounds!" He continued, "Have you dumped your lunch yet Son?"

To which Big Guy replied, " Not yet Dad."

Devereaux said, "Don't get locked up down hole son. We need to get you some fruit; the last thing we need is for you to get sick."

Devereaux was the product of parents who had grown up during a time when regularity was the measure of good health. Devereaux spoke of the various concoctions sold by traveling medicine salesmen when he was a child. He related the fact that his parents thought that a good intestinal cleansing was a necessity in the springtime of the year. So just like cleaning out the garage and tidying up the garden, Devereaux endured a whole bottle of *Triple S Tonic* every spring to help cleanse his bowels of any buildup, which may have occurred since the previous year.

In addition to Devereaux's exposure to patent medicines, he understood the terminology of the oil industry. As an industrial electrician, much of Devereaux's work experience had taken place in the oil fields of Southern California. Terms like "Locked up down hole", were a common term that could be as easily applied to constipation as it could to oil extraction.

To Devereaux life was a collection of jerry rigged solutions, applied in the proper combination to fix any problem, expressed in extemporaneous phrases spontaneously created in his wild mind. When Devereaux spoke, it was as if he was relating a parable. Between the lines of those parables, one could find the context and a deeper meaning of life from Devereaux's point of view. Devereaux was indeed a wise man, but only to those who took the time to read between the lines.

It was interesting to note that Devereaux began to slow down once they had made it to Washington State. They actually stopped at various spots along the highway, including a side tour to see a piece of land near the small town of Raymond that Devereaux had almost purchased back in 1946. The property was a piece of land, about 50 acres in all, half in pasture and half in timber. Devereaux had the means to actually purchase the land at the time, but chose instead to save his money for more "important" things which might have arisen in the future. As Devereaux showed Big Guy the property, his eyes looked longingly back to a place he had always wanted to be, but could never quite reach. The landscape of his heart was often considered by Devereaux to be unrealistic territory, unsuited to a working man with kids to feed. Later in life it was this resignation of his father to a life unfulfilled that caused Big Guy to always seek the "road less taken".

It was late afternoon when they reached Pier 54 in Seattle. Devereaux parked the Volkswagen and they proceeded along Alaskan Way until Big Guy saw a crowd of people gathered around a simple storefront. Above the storefront were the words "Ivars Acres of Clams." Behind the counter was a busy crew dashing here and there to supply the constant demand of the customers who lined up into the street. There taking orders was Ivar Haglund himself. It was interesting to note that Ivar did not write down any of the several orders that he would take at one time.

Instead, he would simply remember each order. Even though Devereaux and Big Guy stood in a large group Ivar could differentiate between those customers who had already ordered and those who were waiting to order. To Big Guy's amazement, when the orders came up from the grill, Ivar would deliver the order to the right customer as he received their payment.

Big Guy ordered scallops and clam strips, while Devereaux ordered fish and chips and clam chowder. With their hands full, they proceeded to a table near the water. No sooner had they sat down, when the local seagulls arrived to beg for scraps. It was a familiar and exciting place to be; in a busy harbor enjoying good seafood in the company of Devereaux. It reminded Big Guy of the times he and his father had spent down in Long Beach Harbor.

After eating at Ivars, Devereaux and Big Guy loaded up and headed east across the floating bridge over Lake Washington on Interstate 90. As they climbed up into the Cascade Mountains, Big Guy could see snow on the mountaintops. The Cascades were covered with evergreens that were interrupted by rocky chutes, which in winter were the pathways for avalanches. The interstate was a marvel, creating a somewhat surreal landscape of highway as sculpture.

As they neared the summit of Snoqualmie Pass, Big Guy could see that the landscape was changing from the cool wet forests of the west side, to the drier pine forests of the east slopes. Devereaux rolled down the window and proclaimed, "Smell the pretty trees!"

It was hard not to notice the fresh scent of evergreen as a blast of wind came rushing in through the open window. "I just love that smell", Devereaux said with a wide grin.

Soon they came into Cle Elum, Washington where they stopped at a hamburger stand and had burgers for dinner. Before they left town they stopped at a grocery store and bought ice, milk and cereal for breakfast. It was getting dark when they got back onto the highway. As they cleared the town limits, they saw deer browsing at the side of the road.

"You better keep an eye out for deer Big Guy", Devereaux said as a deer crossing sign appeared on the right. "I knew a guy from Pennsylvania who spoke about a family that was driving down the turnpike back there when all of a sudden a Whitetail buck ran in front of him. The buck tried to jump over his hood but the guy hit the deer head on with his windshield and the bucks hoof came right through the windshield and pierced his chest."

Big Guy listened to Devereaux's story, wide eyed and amazed. "Did he live?" he asked.

"The guy lived, but to this day I always keep an eye out for deer when I'm driving after dark", Devereaux replied. "So you keep your eyes peeled Piggies and let me know if you see any deer crossing the road". Big Guy spent the rest of that trip exceedingly alert for the first sign of deer crossing the road.

Soon they came to a junction in the road and a sign that said "To US Hwy 97 and Wenatchee". On the east side of the junction was a wide spot in the road with an outhouse and a garbage can. Devereaux pulled off the road and said, "This looks like a good place to stay tonight."

It was pitch black as they settled in for the night, both of them rustling around in the cramped seats. As Devereaux began to snore, Big Guy found that he could not fall asleep. Moreover, as he looked out into the black space that surrounded them, Big Guy became aware of the fact that he had never lived in a place without streetlights. The darkness of this place became Big Guy's first revelation of the beauty of the rural sky at night. As the night revealed itself to him, Big Guy realized how much he had missed in his life. Soon he could hear the calls of a nearby group of coyotes howling at the stars; stars that spread across the sky in a glowing cloud of light. "It must be like this on many nights here" he thought to himself as a peaceful sleep soon overcame him and the endless canopy of starlight enveloped them on that silent dark road, so far from the shore of the Pacific Ocean where he was born.

The sun was just breaking over the horizon; glistening in the sap on the needles of the pine trees above them. The air was full of the sound of birds, as a pair of Steller's Jays arrived with a ruckus. Their constant screeching brought Big Guy up in his seat, as he shook off the stiffness in his joints from sleeping in such a cramped space once again.

Before he knew it, Devereaux was breaking out the cereals, as Big Guy grabbed the plastic bowls and spoons that he had packed.

"It's kid kringles for us this morning Big Guy", Devereaux said as he handed Big Guy the milk. Big Guy sat there eating his cereal and watching a light breeze filter through the pine trees above them.

"These trees are different than the ones over by Seattle", Big Guy said to Devereaux.

"It's drier over here" Devereaux replied. "Where we headed today Dad", Big Guy asked.

"We're heading for the Sheep Ranch", Devereaux replied.

"The Sheep Ranch?" Big Guy asked. "Yep we own a sheep ranch now, didn't I tell you? It's over in Douglas County."

Big Guy had no idea what Devereaux was talking about at the time. Devereaux didn't know anything about sheep and neither did Big Guy, but the thought of owning a place that was open and far from the crowds of Los Angeles County sounded good to him.

Soon they were on the road again climbing higher into the mountains. It was a wild and beautiful place as a Forest Service sign appeared by the roadside, welcoming them to the Wenatchee National Forest. The winding two-lane highway followed a rushing stream to the top of Blewitt Pass. As they crossed the pass several log trucks passed by and Devereaux said, "There must be a mill around here somewhere".

As they drove along, they passed a small white sign on a fence post that featured a smiling worm coming out of an apple that said "Tiny's Cashmere". Big Guy said to Devereaux "Did you see that sign Dad, it had a worm coming out of an apple and said Tiny's."

Devereaux replied, "Tiny's- that's a fruit stand up here in Cashmere, we will have to get some apples there".

They followed the winding highway along another fast flowing stream until they reached the intersection of U.S. Highway 2. Big Guy noticed that they were surrounded by orchards that spread out in all directions. This was indeed a fruit growing region and the neat rows of apple and pear trees framed by the scenic mountains and rushing streams made for a picture postcard scene.

Soon they arrived in the town of Cashmere and sure enough on the left was a big sign that featured the picture of a smiling worm coming out of a bright red apple, a large arrow pointing down and the words "Tiny's Fruit Stand". As they walked into the crude wooden structure, they found rows of tables with baskets of fruit. The smell of fruit was everywhere, and one couldn't help noticing the jars of preserves and packages of fruit candy that decorated the walls in all directions. Soon Devereaux had filled two sacks with Red Delicious Apples.

"Are you ready to go Big Guy?" Devereaux asked.

"Ready when you are Dad." Big Guy replied.

After paying for the apples Devereaux took one and bit into it as he handed Big Guy a sack and they headed back to the Volkswagen to continue their journey. Those apples were some of the best that Big Guy had ever eaten, as they snapped with every bite that he took. "Aren't those good apples?" Devereaux asked. He continued, "Those should keep you regular Aardvark-eat as many as you want.

Soon they found themselves approaching the town of Wenatchee on the banks of the Columbia River in North Central Washington State. Every town needs to have a welcome sign and Wenatchee was no exception.

"Entering Wenatchee- the Apple Capital of the World", were the words that welcomed them to this small town nestled in a green, orchard filled valley. Wenatchee was located at the confluence of the fast flowing Wenatchee River and the Columbia River.

Wenatchee was bordered on the west by high, snow- capped mountains. Big Guy watched as they passed by rows of neat, wood framed houses surrounded by flowering trees and tidy vegetable gardens. Big Guy knew that he had made it to the special place that his father had spoken of for all those years and it was everything that he had imagined it to be.

The sun was shining brightly as they pulled into a service station in Wenatchee. Devereaux filled the gas tank as Big Guy washed the windows. After Devereaux filled the gas tank, he checked the oil and they were on their way. Before they left town they stopped at a Safeway to buy some provisions for the trip to the "Sheep Ranch". Soon they crossed a bridge over the Columbia River into the town of East Wenatchee. East Wenatchee was like a rural cousin to the main town of Wenatchee, an area of scattered homes, fruit warehouses and orchards.

As they drove north through town along the Columbia River, Big Guy noticed that the landscape was becoming even drier as the orchards hugged the river below high basalt bluffs. As they drove past scattered family fruit stands and tidy well-kept orchards, they saw flocks of Canada Geese down in the river as a Red Tailed Hawk circled high above them. Before long, they were entering the town of Orondo and turning onto U.S. Highway 2 as they headed up Pine Canyon towards the Columbia Plateau and the town of Waterville.

After a winding drive up Pine Canyon, they finally made their way out onto the vast wheat fields of the Columbia Plateau. It was a landscape of dark basalt, that had been sculpted by walls of flood water and ancient ice sheets a thousand feet high and hundreds of miles wide, the result of the repeated collapse of prehistoric ice dams in Western Montana several millennia before.

Soon they entered the town of Waterville. Waterville resembled any town in North Dakota, as its tree-lined streets formed a refuge from the constant wind, which blew from all directions. There was something beautiful about Waterville, something simple and sweet; it was a place that lived somewhere in the past, like a black and white photograph of lost loved ones, smiling on that warm day long ago, forever frozen in the glow of the moment.

It was 3:00 on a sunny April afternoon in 1968 as Devereaux and Big Guy drove east on

U.S. Highway 2. They drove through a patchwork of wheat fields in a Volkswagen bug toward a destination unknown. Devereaux was studying an obscure, photocopied map with fuzzy legal descriptions and peculiar road numbers. After a few miles, they came to an intersection and a sign that said simply "Farmer".

The whole community of Farmer consisted of an old grange hall, some grain elevators and an outhouse. As they neared the intersection of Highway 172, they saw a sign that pointed north and included the name of a town called Mansfield.

They turned north onto Highway 172 and continued for four miles until they reached a dirt road with the nondescript name of "4 Road NW." They followed the 4 Road NW until they reached "Rd A NW" where they turned left. It would appear that they were becoming more lost with every turn. Near the corner of Road A NW and 4 1/2 Rd NW, was a pretty little farmhouse with a nice barn and two combines parked out back. It seemed strange to Big Guy that a home so far removed from civilization could be inhabited. They turned right onto 4 1/2 Rd NW and continued east and north up through a little canyon until they reached a wheat field at the intersection of North Division Rd where they turned left.

After a short distance where the road seemed more wheat field than road, they turned right onto 5 Road NE.

After several more miles, they turned right onto Road D NE and stopped. The Volkswagen had pieces of sagebrush stuck in the wheel wells and mud splattered all over its sides and windshield. Devereaux studied the map intently as his powers of orientation were now being tried by a landscape where accurate maps existed only in the minds of those who harvested the fields that surrounded them.

Devereaux knew what Big Guy was thinking when he pointed to the poorly defined plat map and said, "I'm not sure but I think we're here." A smudge marked the spot.

The sun was starting to wane in the western sky when they got out of the cramped Volkswagen and started to walk around. Big Guy was not sure what they were looking for on that sunny afternoon back in 1968. Perhaps Devereaux was thinking that they would see a sign pointing at the ground with the words "Sheep Ranch" written on it. That afternoon, on their first try they never did find the four acres.

****

It was getting dark by the time they got back to the Volkswagen. The sky burned with red and purple tinted clouds as the lone songs of Meadowlarks floated on the breeze. In this unique place, punctuated by an immense silence and the smell of sun-drenched sagebrush, Devereaux and Big Guy sat sipping warm water from a milk jug. Big Guy had spent his entire life surrounded by the drone of the Los Angeles Basin and had never been exposed to a silence of that magnitude before. It was a timeless silence that was at first unnerving, then soon to become soothing to Big Guy's ears. Like the song of the Meadowlarks that called from the worn fence posts that lined the forgotten country road they had followed to get there, there was a rhythm to this remote place that was as ancient as the basalt cliffs that framed the horizon.

Devereaux was frustrated and more than a little irritated that he could not find the land that day. Therefore, they retraced their steps back along the nondescript roads to Highway 172 towards Orondo where they spent the night in a little park next to the road.

Early the next morning Devereaux and Big Guy awoke to the sound of Robins in the park. After a bowl of cereal they washed up and started south on U.S. Highway 2 towards East Wenatchee. Soon after that, U.S. Highway 2 became Highway 28 and then Highway 281 until they reached Interstate 90 near the town of George, Washington.

Soon they were driving across the Mercer Island floating bridge heading into Seattle where they spent the night in a cheap hotel on North Aurora Avenue. It rained off and on all night and in the morning, they loaded up and once again headed south. As the miles passed Devereaux and Big Guy talked about anything and everything. They talked about the Sheep Ranch, the price of gasoline, the price of a loaf of bread during the depression and the life Devereaux lead as a youngster. As Devereaux spoke about his youth, the conversation soon came around to the subject of his father, Frank Meehan.

"You would have loved your grandfather", Devereaux said with a smile.

"What was grandpa like?" Big Guy asked.

"Old Grandpa Snazzy was quite the guy. I will never be half the man he was", Devereaux's face turned somber. "Your grandpa was a man who could say a lot in a few words; he wasn't loud and obnoxious like your Dad. One time after I did something that made him mad, I can't even remember what it was now, it made Old Grandpa Snazzy angry to the point where he was chasing me to give me a spanking. The only problem was that Old Grandpa Snazzy liked to have a beer now and then and his belly did not allow him to run very fast. So there we were, me running down the street and your grandfather Frank Devero trying to catch me. Eventually he stopped running and then he was bent over trying to catch his breath for the next 5 minutes. I kind of felt sorry for him so I quit running. I got what was coming to me in the end but I will never forget him trying to catch me. It was then that I realized that he was getting older."

Devereaux's eyes were misty, as he looked back on a relationship that ended all too soon.

Grandpa Frank had been an electrical inspector for the city of Long Beach back in the 1930s.

Devereaux continued, "One day he was inspecting a warehouse down in the harbor. The warehouse was full of raw lumber from Central America. As your grandfather Frank maneuvered through the stacks of lumber to inspect the wiring in the warehouse, a bug dropped onto his face and before he could brush it off, the bug bit him on the face. The year was 1936, and in 1938 Grandfather Frank had suffered and died from the Chagas Disease, a disease that had been carried by that bug. Back in those days, no one in the medical community had a very good idea of the nature of the Chagas Virus."

Devereaux was 16 years old when his father passed away and the loss haunted Devereaux for the rest of his life. Discussions like this cemented the relationship between Devereaux and his son. Perhaps it was in the telling that one generation hands the past and all the knowledge that it represents onto the next generation. Big Guy loved those discussions with Devereaux who enjoyed them as well. Two days later Big Guy was back in school and daydreaming about Humptulips.

Chapter 4

The Times They Are a Changing

Devereaux and Priscilla were starting to drift apart, as their family seemed to be disintegrating before their eyes. Big Guy remembered helping Devereaux brew beer in the kitchen during those times. As the malt boiled Big Guy would ready the 5- gallon crock. Devereaux would stir the boiling wort on the stove top in a large turkey roasting pan. The aroma of hops and malt would fill the house late into the night. After the wort cooled, Devereaux would transfer it to the 5 gallon crock, which he covered with a round plywood lid, after he measured the specific gravity by adding a bobbing hygrometer.

After a few weeks, Devereaux and Big Guy would siphon the brew into quart bottles that Devereaux had collected and sterilized. After a few batches, the garage was stacked to the rafters with cases of home brew. Moreover, during the summer of 1968, Big Guy recalled many a hot Friday and Saturday night when Devereaux would sit in the dark in his boxer shorts, listening to vinyl recordings of the then famous crooner John Gary, as he drank several quarts of his home brew. Later Big Guy's brothers sought revenge for the loss of their

Beatles albums when they sailed Devereaux's John Gary album over the back fence.

While Priscilla was off to some church function, old Devereaux drank quarts of beer and sang to himself, as his sons handed out cases of home brew to their friends in the driveway. During these nights Big Guy stayed out late, carousing with a few friends, until they were called into their houses by their parents, leaving Big Guy alone to ponder the night.

One day after work, Devereaux asked Big Guy if he wanted to go and check out a used car. Big Guy was excited to go with his dad, as used car shopping was always an adventure with Devereaux. As it turned out this used car expedition was no exception. As they arrived at the address where the used car was, Big Guy noticed a strange foreign car parked in the driveway.

"What kind of car is that?" Big Guy asked.

Devereaux replied, "That is a German car called a Prinz."

"It looks like a Fiat," Big Guy replied.

Devereaux and Big Guy parked in front of the house and walked over to the little green car. Big Guy noticed that it was lacking a rear window. Devereaux pointed out the fact that it was also missing the rear hood, which covered the engine compartment. About that time, the owner walked out of the house and introduced himself to Devereaux.

"What can I tell you about it?" the owner asked.

"How many miles does it have on it?" Devereaux asked.

"It's gone around about once." The man replied.

"Is it OK if we take it for a spin?" Devereaux asked.

"Sure here are the keys. It will run a little rough when you first start it but after it warms up it'll run just fine." The man said.

Devereaux and Big Guy jumped into the little car and Devereaux started the engine. The engine started with a roar and proceeded to sputter at a high RPM; finally slowing down after about a minute.

Devereaux shifted the little car into first gear and moved forward. They drove down the street and came to a stop at a stop sign. "The brakes are a little worn out", Devereaux said. Devereaux continued, "I bet this little car gets good gas mileage".

Big Guy could see the wheels turning in his father's head and knew instantly that Devereaux was going to purchase another used vehicle. "How much does he want for this car?" Big Guy asked.

"He wants $500, but I will see if I can Jew him down to $250", Devereaux replied.

The next day Devereaux and Uncle Don picked up the Prinz and brought it home. The little car entertained Devereaux for about three months. He spent his weekends puttering with it; replacing spark plug wires, fuel filters, and adjusting the carburetor. At one point, the linkage to the throttle came apart, leaving the gas pedal inoperative. This situation did not deter Devereaux from driving the Prinz. He just gerry rigged some baling wire from the throttle lever on the carburetor and passed the bailing wire into the back seat of the car through the missing rear window.

One Saturday evening, after Devereaux had finished a couple of quarts of home brew, he asked Big Guy if he wanted to go for a drive in the Prinz.

"Sure I'll go!" Big Guy replied.

"That's good because I need someone to work the throttle", Devereaux said with a smile.

Before long, the two of them were negotiating the streets of the neighborhood as if using two people to operate one vehicle was an everyday occurrence.

"Okay Big Guy as soon as this signal turns green and I shift into first, I need you to pull on the throttle," Devereaux shouted over his right shoulder.

"Okay Dad!" Big Guy excitedly replied.

As the signal turned green and Devereaux shifted the Prinz into first gear, Big Guy gave a tug on the baling wire and the little car lurched forward. As it gained speed, Devereaux told Big Buy to let up on the throttle as he shifted into second. As Devereaux let up on the clutch, Big Guy once again pulled up on the baling wire and the two of them zoomed down Bellflower Boulevard like an Oklahoma stock car.

In the spring of 1969, Devereaux's two oldest sons had moved out of the house, leaving Big Guy's sister Sheila and his brother Brian in the house. There had been a constant irritation between Devereaux and Priscilla for quite some time over the subject of Priscilla wanting to go back to school to complete the college education that she had always wanted to attain. Devereaux did not want to pay for an education for someone who "didn't need to make a living". Devereaux did not understand that the world had changed; that husbands like him were not in charge anymore. Priscilla was intelligent enough to understand that women were assuming a different roll within society. She came to understand that her meter was running, that time was growing short and that it was time to act.

One afternoon while Priscilla was making enchiladas in the kitchen, angry and enclosed within the one room in the house, which represented all that chained her to the loss and limitations of the past. She allowed her anger to cloud her judgment and while she fumed at the thought of Devereaux's harsh attitude toward her plans; she poured the hot oil that she had used to fry tortillas into a glass mayonnaise jar. Within seconds the jar disintegrated, spilling hot oil onto the kitchen floor. As Priscilla jumped back to escape the burning oil, she lost her footing and slipped. She fell to the floor, her leg crushed and broken in several places from the force of the fall. As she hit the floor and slid toward the cabinets, she was trying to break her fall with her right hand, only to have the jagged shards of glass sever the main artery in her right wrist.

Big Guy was in the other room watching King Kong on the television when he heard the sound of breaking glass along with a loud thud and Devereaux rushing toward the kitchen. "Dear God!" Devereaux screamed in a tone of voice that Big Guy had never heard before. It was the sound of terror, fear in a man who seemed utterly fearless. Soon thereafter Big Guy's brother Brian ran toward the kitchen.

Devereaux just kept screaming, "Dear God!" As Big Guy rose to his feet and walked over to the kitchen, nothing could prepare him for what he saw next. It was his mother lying in a pool of blood on the kitchen floor in a state of shock; her right leg contorted in the most brutal way from the side of her body. Devereaux was holding her wrist in his hand.

Every time that he would ease his grip on her wrist, the blood would spurt freely from the severed artery. Within this cauldron of pain and terror, Devereaux held on, in spite of his own fear of blood he held on. Brian ran to the telephone and dialed the operator. "We need an ambulance!" he yelled. "3508 Tulane Ave, my mom is bleeding." Within minutes, the ambulance arrived and the first responders managed to pry Devereaux's grip from Priscilla's bloody wrist. Big Guy last saw his mother that day, tied at every major joint with tourniquets, strapped to a backboard and placed in the ambulance. The ambulance sped away with Devereaux in hot pursuit. Big Guy spent that terrible day crying alone in his bedroom not sure, if Priscilla was still alive. Big Guy never watched King Kong again.

Priscilla spent the better part of the next year lying in a hospital bed in the living room.

Devereaux was concerned that she would grow too accustomed to being "taken care of", although there was no better caregiver than Devereaux. As summer turned to fall, Priscilla soon enrolled in night classes at Long Beach City College. The world had changed and Devereaux could do nothing about it. Devereaux would drive Big Guy and Priscilla to the campus, and Big Guy would follow his mom as she walked with the aid of crutches to her classes, carrying her books and helping her where he could. Big Guy remembered those warm nights, when moths swarmed the campus streetlights and his mind, exhilarated by the potential of the expanding world around him, raced with excitement at the wonder of it all.

During those wonderful days of youth Big Guy studied everything with excitement. At that time he was torn between becoming an entomologist and studying oceanography. On those warm nights, Big Guy would ride in his Brother Brian's low rider to the sounds of Creedence Clearwater Revival on the eight-track player. They cruised south along Pacific Coast Highway to visit Brian's future wife Chris at Sunset Beach, where she lived with her aunt and uncle. It was during the red tides, when the nighttime sea glowed in a bio luminescent blue light. As Big Guy walked along the beach, every footstep left a glowing blue shadow in the shimmering sand. The waves rolled in as blue tunnels; as the moment seeped into Big Guy's subconscious, as seductive as in later years and the first time Big Guy ever made love (on that very same beach).

Devereaux cooked Thanksgiving Dinner that year. While the Meehans all sat down at the dining room table and gave thanks for what they had, Priscilla ate dinner in her hospital bed, being served by her family and enjoying it immensely. After dinner Devereaux asked if anyone wanted to ride with him to take his Grandma Ethel back to her home downtown. As usual, no one wanted to accompany Devereaux except Big Guy. Grandma Ethel was an amazing woman, who had been born and raised in a mining camp in the Superstition Mountains of the Arizona Territory in the latter half of the nineteenth century. As they drove, Big Guy always asked his grandma questions about life "back in the old days". To which she would let her mind wander back and the stories would pour forth. They were amazing tales of hardship, class warfare and some good old- fashioned Irish blarney. On their way back from grandma's Devereaux drove to the top of Signal Hill, where they often went and watched the sunset.

Devereaux would relate the tales of his own childhood growing up in the neighborhoods below them.

As the sun sank into the Pacific Ocean, Big Guy asked Devereaux, "What was it like when the earthquake struck back in 1933?"

To which he replied, "It was close to six o'clock and we were about to eat dinner. Everyone was seated at the table and we were about to eat beef meat and red chili. Then all hell broke loose and we all held on until the house started to shift. Dishes were falling out of the cupboards as the walls around us started to crack with an awful sound. The shaking seemed to last forever. Fearing that the house would fall on us, we ran outside. My three sisters were crying as my mom and dad just stared at each other in disbelief from the curb. Soon I realized that I had left my cigar box in the house. The cigar box had all the money that I had saved in it. You know your Dad- Mr. Bennefeld the Fairfax Indian- I ran back into the house, grabbed my cigar box and ran back out-just as the whole house slid off its foundation. After the shaking stopped, people in the neighborhood were milling around in the street in confusion. Rumors were flying that a tidal wave was heading for town.

We made our way up here to Signal Hill and waited to see if it would come. It was crowded up here that night. There must have been 500 people up here. It was kind of funny; there were different people all crowded together up here that night- rich and poor, Mexicans and white people. They were all happy to still be alive and it didn't matter who they were standing next to that night. We had campfires and waited until the next day to go back to what was left of our homes." Devereaux paused with a smile and then related the story of a drunken sailor who was standing in the crowd who exclaimed that he had "Never seen a tidal wave arrive on time yet!"

"Fairfax Indian?" Big Guy asked. "Oh just my Jewish side showing itself", Devereaux explained with a smile. Once again Devereaux reverted back to the comfortable stereotypes that he grew up with. Big Guy just shook his head.

As they stared out over the broad expanse of the Pacific Ocean, Bid Guy could not help but think about the wide expanse of grass and the Sheep Ranch that they had tried to find back in April.

"Do you think we will ever find the four acres", Big Guy asked Devereaux.

"We'll find it", Devereaux replied with a smile.

It was getting dark when Devereaux started the Volkswagen and headed toward Hill Street.

Hill Street was a steep stretch of road that locals would use to test the power of their cars and trucks. It was one of the few streets in the Long Beach Area that required lower gears to negotiate. Hill Street was also the most direct way down from the top of Signal Hill to the rest of the city. As they reached the edge of the grade, Devereaux shifted the Volkswagen into second gear and lifted his foot off the brake pedal. The engine on the little Volkswagen strained as they drove down the grade at a slow pace. Devereaux said, "This little bug has great compression."

As they drove along Willow Street through the tunnel that passed under the airport runways, Devereaux blew the horn and smiled, so ending a typical Sunday night during Big Guy's youth.

Two months later and without Big Guy, Devereaux returned to Washington with his brother Don, and after consulting with a local wheat farmer named Francis Hicks, they finally located the 4 acres that he and Big Guy had tried to locate earlier that year. Farmer Hicks was a quiet man who did not quite know what to make out of this loud, animated man from the big city.

The locals like Francis Hicks, knew the four acres as "The Triangle", as it was the only 4-acre triangle in the county to their knowledge.

After walking around the four acres with Devereaux and Don, pointing out the boundaries as if he had an internal compass, Farmer Hicks explained the characteristics of the soil, the annual weather patterns and the depth that a well had to be drilled to find water. Devereaux liked Farmer Hicks right off as he inquired about the possibility of farming the four acres, which had always been virgin land.

"How many bushels of wheat do you think that I could get off this land?", Devereaux asked.

Farmer Hicks looked surprised as he thought for a moment.

"It would be pretty good for a few years", farmer Hicks replied.

Then he quickly followed up, "I could farm it for you, but why would you want me to?"

Devereaux looked confused, as he had not become fully acquainted with this unique piece of land that he had purchased.

Farmer Hicks continued, "If I farmed it you would no longer have the wildflowers in the spring, like the Shooting Stars and the little yellow Buttercups. I can farm it, but think about it awhile and then let me know." Devereaux never did farm the four acres.

Later that year, Big Guy was once again back at Saint Cornelius Catholic School. He did not figure that he would be getting the chance to accompany Devereaux back to "God's Country" anytime soon.

****

It was late July in the summer of 1969, when Devereaux told Big Guy that he was going back up to Washington to visit the four acres. It was with great excitement that Big Guy asked him if he could go as well.

"Get your stuff", Devereaux said as he proceeded to load up the Volkswagen bug with supplies.

Once again, they were on the road, two travelers from different generations looking for God's Country in a Volkswagen Bug.

The San Joaquin and Sacramento valleys were a blur as they headed north. It was not until they reached the town of Weed, California that Big Guy realized that they were taking a different route than they had taken the last time. This new route took them north into Central Oregon through the towns of Klamath Falls, Bend, Redmond and Madras.

Perhaps the reason that the first leg of their journey was such a blur was the fact that they had left Long Beach at 11:00 at night and were proceeding to drive straight through. After a few roadside catnaps, Devereaux forged ahead arriving in Central Oregon after dark on the second night. They arrived at a rest area just south of Madras named after the explorer Peter Skene Ogden.

As they pulled off into the pitch-blackness of the Central Oregon night Big Guy stepped out to use the restroom and was once again amazed by the ceiling of stars that encompassed them on that night. It seemed strange to Big Guy; here it was the middle of summer yet this place was as cold as the coldest winter in Southern California. A cool evening breeze carried the scent of Juniper as they settled into a rather chilly night's rest in the front seats of the VW bug. It was cold in this strange new place, as the high desert of Central Oregon always is during the clear nights year round.

The next morning Big Guy awoke to the sounds of Devereaux arranging the camp supplies in the back seat. It was not long before he was scrambling to find his jacket, which Big Guy managed to pick up at the last minute just before they left home two nights before.

Even more amazing was the sight of a deep gorge only a few feet away from the Volkswagen bug. As Big Guy walked over and peered over the edge, there before him was a dark basalt canyon. The dark canyon walls had patches of yellow-green lichens and it looked as though the canyon had been carved by water. Far down below in the bottom of the canyon was a fast flowing river. Swallows darted around the two-lane, highway bridge that crossed the gorge at this point. A warm breeze touched Big Guy face, as he watched a Golden Eagle soar above the canyon.

Devereaux asked if he wanted some breakfast. "Did you see this deep canyon over here Dad?" Big Guy asked. Devereaux walked over and put his arm around his son.

"What do you think of that Big Guy?" Devereaux inquired.

"I wonder what made this canyon." Big Guy mumbled to himself as he wondered about the forces that created it.

"Probably that river down there", Devereaux replied pointing down at the churning Crooked River below.

After they ate breakfast they were on the road again heading north on Highway 97. After climbing up a steep canyon, they came to a junction in the road with a sign that pointed the way to two distinct paths, in this case Portland or Shaniko. Everyone has encountered junctions like this one in their travels; decision points regarding their fate and everything that such decisions represent. Maupin Junction has always served as a reminder to Big Guy of the power of choice. To Big Guy it would always represent an opportunity to choose the path less traveled.

After turning towards Shaniko, the landscape opened up into a wide expanse of rolling hills, sagebrush and wheat fields. Bordered on the west by the symmetrical, snow covered peaks of the Cascade Range; they had entered a place more different from any that Big Guy had ever known.

Big Guy had never driven on a road with so few people or settlements. As the landscape passed by and the shadows of clouds raced along the road, they came to the ghost town of Shaniko. Oregon. Shaniko was in reality a collection of the skeletons of buildings that lined the streets of a once prosperous sheep-shipping center. The sheep were all gone; replaced by wandering dogs, the singing wind and a world where live sheep seldom ride on trains any more.

Soon they were driving down a winding canyon. It was as if they were traveling through a landscape that was anticipating the encounter of something larger down the road. Around the next bend in the road, they encountered Biggs Junction and the mighty Columbia River.

It was the first time that Big Guy had ever seen the Columbia River and he was taken aback by the sheer size of it. The dark basalt cliffs that formed its channel, looked as if they had been cut by some incredible ancient force, long forgotten by time. Big Guy looked out the window of the VW and wondered why a world with such violent geological signs, could be so benign today. Seagulls circled in a freshening breeze as they stopped in a gas station in Biggs and filled up the tank. Biggs, Oregon was an important junction on Interstate 84 and Highway 97. Its important location had served as a way point to travelers for thousands of years. As soon as the car had stopped, Big Guy jumped out of the cramped VW and proceeded to wipe the windows much to the surprise of the gas station attendant who was about ready to initiate that task. Big Guy learned that in Oregon, attendants pump the gas for you and cleaned windshields are usually included.

After checking the oil, Devereaux paid cash for the gasoline and they once again continued their journey north. Devereaux always paid cash for stuff. He believed that there was something inherently dishonest about credit and it was a rare occasion when he used a credit card. In fact, it was Priscilla who explained that he would not have a very good credit rating because he did not have a credit card. A point that Devereaux learned the hard way when he applied for his first gasoline credit card and was turned down because he had always paid his debts in full with cash.

As they drove over the bridge separating Oregon and Washington, Big Guy looked down on the power of the river as it formed waves on its way to the Pacific Ocean.

"There's the mighty sea", Devereaux proclaimed.

"Not too many rivers as big as that one", he said with a smile.

Soon they were winding their way up to the top of Satus Pass. The hillsides were covered with Ponderosa pine and White Oak. To Big Guy, the White Oaks looked as much out of place as a Douglas-fir would look, growing in the middle of the Sonoran Desert. It was strange to see oak trees in this area when he had not seen them anywhere else. Here and there they saw old cabins, and ranch buildings that had long ceased to be inhabited; forgotten testaments to timeless old dreams and opportunities that had ended abruptly.

Then Big Guy saw it, "Look Dad! Look at the sign on the fence post- there's that worm coming out of the apple!" Big Guy exclaimed.

Devereaux replied, "That's Tiny's - Cashmere!"

It was the same sign that Big Guy had seen the last time that they were driving north a year ago.

"What is it doing on the fence clear out here", Big Guy asked.

"Just advertising", Devereaux replied.

As they drove on Big Guy noticed a golden eagle soaring high in the sky; circling as though it was looking for something. Round and round it soared as Big Guy's mind wandered; imagining that he was that eagle looking down at the earth below and reveling in the freedom of flight.

It was late afternoon and they were driving along a steep and winding stretch of Highway 821 heading north toward Ellensburg. This stretch of road followed the Yakima River and was treacherous enough to cause Devereaux to sit up and pay closer attention to his driving. As they neared the bottom of the last grade, they came across several vehicles stopped in the road. As Devereaux slowed the Volkswagen, Big Guy noticed men running towards the bank of the highway. Devereaux pulled the Volkswagen over and got out to see what was going on. Big Guy watched Devereaux walk over to the edge of the road and look down only to quickly walk back to the car.

"Dear God!" He exclaimed, "That was terrible!"

"What was the matter?" Big Guy asked.

"That was a station wagon that went over the side of the road. It was upside down and there were bodies scattered all over the place!"

Big Guy had not seen what Devereaux had saw, but by the tone in his voice, he could tell that it was bad.

"Dear God!" he repeated.

Big Guy had not heard that tone in his voice since his mother's accident, and it unnerved Big Guy. He thought about what his father had just seen and he wondered if there was anything that they could have done to help. As they left that terrible scene, an ambulance passed by with its lights and siren blaring. It seemed that Devereaux was in no place to help.

Pain was something that Devereaux could deal with when it was his own pain. The pain of others was quite a different story.

The drive to Ellensburg was quiet. In Ellensburg, they stopped at a roadside café and Devereaux had a cup of coffee. Big Guy could tell that Devereaux, upset by what he had seen, needed some time to settle down. They spent the night at a wide spot in the road and Big Guy tried hard to forget that day's events.

Big Guy awoke the next morning to a bright ray of sunshine piercing the shade above the dashboard.

"Would you like a sip of coffee Aardvark?" Devereaux asked.

"Let me take a taste." Big Guy replied.

Devereaux handed Big Guy a small cup of coffee and he sipped it thoughtfully.

"How long will it take until we get there?" Big Guy asked.

"We'll get there this afternoon", Devereaux replied.

After driving through a vast, wind-swept country, it was at 2:00 that afternoon when they pulled up to the side of a dirt road east of Mansfield Washington. Devereaux had the nondescript plat map spread out on the hood of the car. His dark eyes scanned the horizon looking for some point of reference that did not exist on the map. Big Guy was more interested in the strange wasp that was flying around a small hole in the ground by his feet. As he looked closer, Big Guy noticed that the wasp had a small beetle in its grip. As he stared, the wasp placed the beetle down into the small hole, and soon disappeared into the sagebrush. There were all sorts of strange insects that lived in this sagebrush steppe. It was a world unique unto itself, where every living thing struggled to survive against long odds.

As Big Guy looked around, he noticed a small, nondescript patch of the sagebrush that had a broken barbed wire fence surrounding it. He wandered over to see why this particular area had a small fence around it. Under the scattered sagebrush, there were several mounds, each one neatly arranged next to the other. Without knowing it, Big Guy had provided Devereaux with a landmark that helped him determine their location.

"That's a graveyard there", Devereaux said. "It's right here on the map. It's an old one- probably over 100 years old."

Big Guy stared at the mounds and pondered the lives of those who were buried there. Only the sagebrush and the earth itself marked that these lives had ever existed.

"I know where we are now", Devereaux said as he jumped back into the VW bug and started the engine. Devereaux turned right onto Road D NE and they charged south in a cloud of rolling dust. After a mile they turned right again and headed west on a road without a sign. After another mile, Big Guy saw an old abandoned house on the left as the road veered sharply to the right. As Devereaux neared the intersection, he cranked the steering wheel hard to the right. The tires of the VW partially slid around the gravel turn as two tracks overgrown with native Ryegrass stretched out before them and rounded a curve to the left. It was as if Devereaux was being chased by the hounds of hell, as he raced down the overgrown road. Within a minute, they came around a curve beneath a gently sloping knoll that was covered in native sagebrush and bunchgrass. Up the two tracks, they charged until they reached the top of the brush-covered knoll. "We're here Piggies -The Sheep Ranch!" Devereaux exclaimed with excitement, as he turned off the engine of the VW.

As Big Guy emerged from the cramped VW, he was struck by an incredible silence and the gentle swaying of the wind in the bunch grass. To most this scene would have been the epitome of anti-climax; nothing more than a sage covered knoll in a vast ocean of empty space. In Big Guy's mind it was a place where one could create something new or at least discover something new about one's self.

Cicadas sang from the sage, in unison with small brush birds that chirped occasionally. Mostly it was the sound of the rushing wind that caught Big Guy's ear, as it bent the bunch grass and sent dust devils spinning on the horizon in all directions. An immense blue sky, punctuated with puffy white cumulus clouds that seemed to reflect the shades of color from the landscape below.

Big Guy turned to find Devereaux wandering toward a distant fence line; Big Guy ran to catch up.

"Where are you going Dad?" Big Guy asked, as the two marched along; solitary figures on a vast, empty grass covered sea.

"This fence is a section line and it is where the starting line begins for figuring where our property starts and stops." Devereaux replied.

He was a man on a mission. Armed with an old rolled up cloth tape measure and some stakes, Devereaux was ready to delineate his little piece of "God's Country."

From the fence line, he began to pace off each chain of measurement, as he rolled out the tape for confirmation. When he came to what he surmised was a corner, he tapped in a wooden stake with the backside of an old hatchet. Soon they were on the far eastern point of the property, where the boundaries formed the point of a flattened triangle.

"You stay here big guy, while I get some more stakes." Devereaux said as he wandered back toward the VW. The land consisted of several knolls, so when Devereaux disappeared over the first knoll, Big Guy was all alone in this vast and silent place. As the silence closed in around Big Guy, his mind began to wander. "I wonder if there are bears here," he thought as his mind contemplated what it meant to be really alone for the first time. As the youngest of six kids in a noisy family where one never seemed to be truly alone, this was a strange and somewhat disconcerting place for Big Guy to be. "Of course there are no bears around here," he said to himself in a half-hearted attempt to reassure himself.

As the minutes pasted and Devereaux did not return, his mind came up with different imaginings that required self-reassurance. Big Guy turned to find a large whirlwind rolling toward him over a plowed field. He stared wide-eyed as it came nearer. Like its larger cousin the tornado, the approaching dust devil rotated violently, as it lofted dark soil, sagebrush limbs and tumbleweeds high into the sky.

"I wonder if Dad sees that whirly wind heading my way." Big Guy thought.

Big Guy was just about ready to call out to Devereaux when he reappeared from over the hill. In one hand, he had a hand full of stakes and in the other; he was carrying a plastic milk jug that was full of hot drinking water.

"How are you doing Pigs? I brought some water- here take a drink." Devereaux handed Big Guy the milk jug.

After he took a long swallow, Big Guy pointed to the dust devil and asked, "Do you see the big whirly wind Dad?"

Just as Devereaux looked over at the dust devil, it dissipated as it cleared the plowed field and hit a large patch of sagebrush. "There are lots of dust devils out here." Devereaux said as he took a long sip of water.

"Did you ever get caught in a Tornado dad?", Big Guy asked.

"Not many tornadoes in Southern California Big Guy." Devereaux replied with a wink.

By the time they finished marking the last corner, it was time to make dinner. Before Big Guy knew it, Devereaux had retrieved the old green Coleman Stove from somewhere behind the seat of the Volkswagen Bug. He unscrewed the cap from the top of the red fuel tank and proceeded to dump white gas into the tank. He then connected the nozzle that extended from the fuel tank to the burners and began to pump the fuel tank full of air. He slowly turned the knob that controlled the flow of fuel vapors into the burner. As the vapors rushed through the burner, Devereaux struck a match and ignited the first burner on the stove. The circle of blue flame gave off a faint petroleum smell as it began to burn cleanly.

Soon Devereaux began to once again rummage through the back of the heavily ladened Volkswagen, where he found the ice chest, and proceeded to pull out two large packages that contained round steaks. Devereaux uncovered the steaks, placing them on a paper plate where he sprinkled salt and pepper on them. Then he took the frying pan and placed it on the burner. Devereaux began to slice up some potatoes and onions; tossing them carefully into the pan along with some butter. After adjusting the heat, he began to stir the potatoes as the smell began to waft over the sage.

"You're going to love this stuff Piggies", Devereaux said with a smile.

"Could you look in the box in the back of the car and grab the can of peas Big Guy?" Devereaux asked. Devereaux pointed to a large stinkbug that was crawling on the ground by Big Guy's feet, "Looks like Good Time Charley is in a hurry to get somewhere." Devereaux said with a smile.

As the beetle scurried away, Devereaux continued cooking the evening meal. Soon the potatoes and onions were cooked to a golden brown. After adding more butter to the pan Devereaux placed the steaks next to each other, as the smell of cooking meat swirled around them. As the steaks sizzled, Devereaux reached into the ice chest and pulled out an ice cold Rainier Beer. He took a long swig, handed it to Big Guy, and said, "Here you go Aardvark, have a taste."

Big Guy tilted the bottle back and took a sip. As long as he could remember, Devereaux had always offered Big Guy a taste of his beer. Whether it was his homebrew or something that he bought at the store, a sip of beer was always offered to the kids. To Big Guy it was no big deal, just an acknowledgment that he was there, experiencing Devereaux's life with him. While he had not acquired a taste for the brew, the cold beverage was quite refreshing.

There was something special about sharing that cold beer with Devereaux; it was just the two of them enjoying each other's company in that isolated place so long ago. It was a timeless experience of one generation passing the nuances of living to the next. To Devereaux there was no wife there to complain, no troublesome children clamoring for his attention. There was only one son there, the one who was willing to accept him as he was.

Soon dinner was ready and they both found a rock to sit on. Devereaux pulled out his pocketknife and cut up the steaks into bite-sized pieces. As Devereaux sipped his beer and the sun began to set, a peaceful glow enveloped the landscape. The sun was setting, wrapped in an explosion of color that radiated out through the brilliant clouds, sending streaks of light to dance on the tips of the sage and swaying grasses. The landscape was transformed into a great cathedral, complete with stained glass windows that brought the light of heaven in contact with the earth. Big

Guy watched the light play across his father's face, as a warm breeze swirled past.

Before it was dark, they decided to take a hike toward the south. As they cleared the very top of the knoll, they saw a coyote. He was trotting right towards them, as the wind was in their faces and he had not spotted them yet. Devereaux stopped Big Guy in his tracks, and as he pointed at the coyote, it suddenly saw them and raced off in the opposite direction. As the coyote disappeared in the sage, they could see a small canyon in the distance.

"That must be Dutch Henry Draw over there", Devereaux said as he pointed toward the south. "That's where that coyote is headed."

"What did you think of that Big Guy?" Devereaux asked. "That was neat!" Big Guy replied.

That night they had a small campfire that consisted of dead sage limbs and dried cow chips. As Big Guy poked at the fire; old Good Time Charley crawled past his shoe and a shooting star zipped across the brilliant night sky.

"Look at the sky Dad!" Big Guy exclaimed. "Look at all the stars!"

The Milky Way was splashed across the sky as star clusters intertwined with galaxies and the landscape glowed in the reflected light. In addition to the silence, Big Guy had never experienced the starlight in such darkness. As the coals in the fire burned red, blue and orange, the lonely howl of coyotes pierced the night silence.

For a whole week on that trip, Devereaux and Big Guy had talked about everything. When at last they crossed the Grapevine and were once again in sight of the glow of the Los Angeles Basin, Big Guy couldn't help but feel sad and somewhat out of place. "The lives of so many people, in such close proximity, how could one live in such a place?" He thought.

Soon they were engulfed in the rush hour traffic of the 405 Freeway. "No one here will ever know where we just came from." Big Guy mused to himself as his thoughts of distant swaying grass soon blended into the taillights of a million different lives; each one removed from the other by time, circumstance and the white lines on the rubber stained pavement.

Chapter 5

There Has to Be Something More to Life Than This.

By 1969 Devereaux's family had partially disintegrated. Every one of his children was doing "their own thing". He and Priscilla had envisioned something different when they had started out back in 1947.

The things that an eleven-year-old boy would consider interesting consumed Big Guy's life. There were also many unique things and ways of looking at the world that encouraged Big Guy to look deeper into the possibilities of life. At the most basic level Big Guy was a dreamer; someone who saw what others could not see. When he looked out at the sea, Big Guy could see himself on a research ship, studying the ocean as an oceanographer. When he looked at an insect, he could see himself in the Amazon Rain Forest, as an entomologist. To Big Guy it was never a question of his ability, it was always a question of choice. It may not have been realistic, but his dreams sustained Big Guy according to the American traditions that had sustained the Meehan's ever since they stepped off the boat on the eastern seaboard of North America back in the 1600's.

It was spring and one morning Devereaux asked Big Guy if he wanted to inspect a vehicle that he had found in the classified ads section of the newspaper.

When they arrived at the address, Big Guy saw a beige Volkswagen camper van parked on the street. Devereaux introduced himself to the owner and proceeded to look under the hood as Big Guy surveyed the interior of the camper van. With 35,000 miles on it, the vehicle proved to be a good deal for $3800.

Before Big Guy knew it, they had purchased a somewhat more comfortable mode of transportation. It was not long before Devereaux was ready to hit the road once again.

To Big Guy's surprise they had company on this trip to the Sheep Ranch. Brian, or "Perkins Pig" as Devereaux nicknamed him, joined the expedition.

Brian was in his late teens, and was then occupied by work and his girlfriend. He looked forward to seeing this "Sheep Ranch" that he kept hearing about. He had managed to get some time off work, and it was summer after all.

As the three travelers motored toward Bakersfield, it became apparent that one of the major drawbacks to a Volkswagen camper bus was the lack of power when it came to passing or climbing a grade. As the heavily burdened camper bus neared the summit of the Grapevine, the speedometer read 30 miles per hour. Passing drivers appeared to be upset as they maneuvered around the slow moving camper van.

When they arrived at the Sheep Ranch it was the middle of July and the fields were curing from green to light brown. The days were long at that latitude, and it was early evening by the time that they reached the Sheep Ranch. Brian stepped out of the camper van and surveyed the vast distances that surrounded them. "This is kind of cool", he said as a warm breeze rustled the sage. It was nine o'clock and the sun was just below the horizon. The day had been warm and towering thunderheads crowded the distant mountains to the west and north. Devereaux started to arrange their camp spot as Brian and Big Guy joined in to build the campfire. Soon Devereaux and Perkins Pig had broken into a half case of Rainier Beer and they were all munching on crackers and cheese.

As darkness rose over the wheat fields that dotted the landscape around them and the edges of the storm clouds glowed with the colors of the sunset; a full moon rose in the east from behind scattered clouds, turning the edges of each to bright silver. In the west and north, the distant clouds began to rattle with thunder as streaks of lightning permeated the interior of each cloud. It was strange that, while the sun had set in the west, the northern horizon was not getting any darker. As a matter of fact, the northern horizon was starting to glow with a strange light.

Devereaux stared off toward the north and commented, "Maybe I have had too many beers, but it looks like it's getting lighter in the north."

Brian noticed the same strange light, as did Big Guy. The campfire crackled and popped as stories passed between the generations. After an hour had passed, all three looked up at an open sky that sparkled with billions of stars; framed by flashes of distant lightning and a widening glow that continued in the northern sky.

"That's the Northern Lights!" Devereaux exclaimed as he gazed north. Native Southern Californians seldom if ever saw a sight such as this.

"Wow!' Brian and Big Guy added simultaneously.

With lightning on the horizon, a full moon above and the light of infinite stars beyond, they stood in awe at the wonder of this spectacle. Shafts of light in all the colors of the rainbow beamed down from a neon like band of light that seemed to encircle the whole width of the northern sky. The shafts of glowing light illuminated the ripening wheat fields, creating even more light. It was as if the whole prairie was entrapped in one great crystal diamond mirror, bursting forth in a flood of light.

The three spectators below were dumb struck. Even Devereaux, never at a loss for words, was struck by the power of the moment. The prairie breeze soon touched their faces, as if the hand of God was taking note of their presence. A sense of awe stirred within them, as this unique vision ebbed and flowed on that special night. All three soon nodded off to sleep, uncertain if that night had all been a dream.

After breakfast the next morning, the three travelers hiked down Dutch Henry Draw until they reached the edge of Moses Coulee. Along the way they encountered Sage Grouse and a herd of Mule Deer bucks.

"What do you think about that Perkins Pig?" Devereaux asked as they watched the deer scatter.

"Are there deer around here?" Brian asked. "No those are horses with horns." Big Guy retorted. To this Brian noogied Big Guy's head and nudged him aside.

As they walked up to the edge of Moses Coulee, Brian peered over the edge of a three hundred foot basalt cliff. It fell abruptly, into a wide, sage filled canyon. Once again, there was this immense geologic feature, shrouded in silence and far removed from civilization. Like a wild living thing, nestled in a forgotten dry place, Moses Coulee was alive with soaring eagles and Peregrine Falcons that swooped and dived above at lightning speed. Devereaux peered through a pair of binoculars across the sage covered coulee, making note of where US Highway 2 crossed to the south and where Jamison Lake was located to the north.

After the trio had drank some water out of the milk jug that Devereaux had carried, they were about to head back up the draw when two A6 military jet aircraft on a low level practice flight roared overhead.

"Holy Shit!" Devereaux exclaimed. "Where in the hell did those come from?"

A short while after the A6 jets passed; a giant B-52 Bomber screamed over about 300 feet above their heads. Devereaux followed the large aircraft with the binoculars; it was camouflage green and making a slow turn toward the north.

"The Air Force must train in this area", Devereaux said as he watched the larger aircraft fade into the distance. The trio continued up Dutch Henry Draw and after exploring some side canyons, soon returned to the camper.

The night was spent once again around the campfire, spinning yarns and telling lies as Devereaux used to say.

"Wasn't grandpa from up here?" Brian asked. "Your granddad was raised down in the Blue Mountains of Northeast Oregon back in the late 1800s. Did I ever tell you boys about the time that your granddad was hunting and he was tracked by a mountain lion?" Devereaux asked.

"No." Big Guy and Brian answered simultaneously.

"One day your granddad was hunting deer and he was following their tracks in the snow. As the day was getting dark, your granddad decided to turn back for home. As he walked back, following the same tracks he hiked in on, he noticed a big cougar print imposed over his own tracks. It looked like that cougar had tracked your granddad for most of the day.

"How did he get from Oregon to California?" Brian asked.

"Well times were tough in NE Oregon and the railroad was expanding up north in Washington, so your granddad headed up to Spokane about 1906. One day he was watching some electrical lineman up on a power pole. Suddenly one of them slipped and fell.

Later that day the foreman was looking to replace the injured linemen. He approached your grandfather, who had continued to hang around asking numerous questions about line work. The foreman asked him if he had ever done electrical work. Your grandpa said that he could do the work without any problem. The foreman looked at your grandfather and said that he didn't ask him if he could do the work he asked him if he had ever DONE the work. Anyway, to make a long story short your granddad was hired on the spot and proved himself to be a very capable lineman. Before long, he became a member of the International Brotherhood of Electrical Workers. Soon the San Francisco earthquake struck and there was a lot of work for electricians down in that part of California. Your grandfather set out for California and worked out of Oakland for about a year.

After that, he moved on to the Salt River Project that was starting down in the Arizona Territory. Salt River was a dam building project that brought water and power to Phoenix in the early years. Your grandfather was a tramp back in those early days in the electrical trade. A tramp was a union electrician who was traveling in search of work. He traveled in railroad boxcars quite a bit. It was down in Arizona that he met your grandmother. He was up on a power pole one day out in your grandmother's backyard in Phoenix. Your grandmother happened to notice him up on the power pole and being that it was a hot day, offered him some cold lemonade. Your old granddad accepted her offer and using his climbing spurs took about two steps and was back on the ground drinking lemonade with his future wife."

They all stared into the glowing coals of the campfire, as a shooting star passed overhead. Like the night before, this night proved to be one of those nights that engaged the generations.

A week later, they were back in Los Angeles County, and Big Guy was in his room dreaming about the wide-open horizon and the dancing northern lights that he had witnessed while camped out on the Sheep Ranch. Big Guy looked out the front window to a world of tract houses, neatly arranged in uniform rows. He walked outside, looked at the sky through the trees in his yard, and wondered if he would ever get the opportunity to leave that place behind. Just then, Devereaux arrived home from work.

Big Guy watched his father come home from work many times in his young life; always tired and dirty from a long, hard day at a job that he might not have cared for much.

Devereaux sat on the front porch, removed his boots and socks before walking into the house.

"How did your work go today dad?" Big Guy asked.

"It was a good day today." Devereaux replied. "We ran a 4 inch conduit to a motor, which required that we bend some pipe and bury it", he continued.

Devereaux wandered back to the bedroom, then Devereaux took his bath and soon came out wearing only his boxer shorts and a T-shirt. As was his daily ritual, he went to the refrigerator and took out a quart of Budweiser and a frozen glass from the freezer. Devereaux retired to his favorite chair where he poured himself a cold one and read the newspaper. After an hour reading the newspaper and drinking his beer, Devereaux was ready for dinner.

"Priscilla?" Devereaux called out.

"Mom is at class I think", Big Guy answered.

"It looks like leftovers tonight", Devereaux replied.

The beer seemed to be taking effect as Devereaux was not very concerned about dinner. Soon he was reheating a pan of spaghetti on the stove. After dinner, Devereaux watched some TV and went to bed, only to start the whole process over again at 5:00 the next morning.

When the weekend arrived, Devereaux was reading the paper in his favorite chair when Big Guy came into the room. "How would you like to check out a new bicycle with me?" Devereaux asked.

"What kind of Bicycle?" Big Guy asked.

"I don't know", Devereaux replied. Maybe we will get a bike for your mom, so we can get her out of that hospital bed. Priscilla was still going to physical therapy, when she was not attending college. While she was still sleeping in the front room in a hospital bed, she was improving with every passing day. The main problem was that while the doctors had managed to save her leg, it was offset at a strange angle from her good leg, which made walking difficult.

Within two hours there were two new bicycles in the driveway. At about that time Priscilla arrived back home from college in the VW bug that Devereaux had recently purchased for her. As she backed up, she almost ran into the new bikes. Stepping out of her car, she surveyed the bicycles and looked suspiciously at Devereaux.

"What do you think Mother Superior?" Devereaux asked.

"I haven't ridden a bicycle in years!" Priscilla exclaimed.

It seemed that Priscilla wasn't going to start riding a bicycle anytime soon, as Big Guy never did see her on the bike that he could recall. Perhaps it was because Devereaux had left her out of the buying process, or that she simply did not like to ride bicycles. This resulted in her bicycle collecting dust in the garage for months. In the end, Big Guy regularly rode the bike with Devereaux to the airport to watch the planes take off and land. Riding bikes became a regular occurrence for Devereaux and Big Guy on summer evenings after dinner.

Chapter 6

There's a Big World Out There

The harbor was Big Guy's window on the world. On the weekends, Devereaux and Big Guy would drive down to Long Beach harbor to look at the ships docked there. By taking Big Guy to the harbor, Devereaux had unwittingly opened up the larger world to his son.

To Big Guy, a bicycle represented freedom. It was the vehicle by which distance could be negotiated by an eleven year old boy. The harbor was a special place, where the world came to visit and Big Guy could travel the world merely by riding his bicycle across town.

One day Big Guy and his friend Johnny rode their bicycles across the city to the harbor. Back in those days, it was not a problem to get close to freighters from around the world. After riding their bicycles 10 miles one way, dodging buses and cars at every intersection, Big Guy and Johnny found themselves standing on a pier gazing up at a freighter from South Korea. The longshoremen were hurrying around in their forklifts, picking up pallets of boxes and moving them into the warehouses that lined the dock. Before long one of the sailors on board the freighter motioned for Big Guy and Johnny to climb up the gangway and board the ship, which was named *The Korean Shepard*. Big Guy and Johnny looked at each other in surprise.

"My mom isn't going to like this." Johnny said as they started up the gangway steps.

As Big Guy and Johnny neared the top of the gangway one of the crew greeted them with handshakes and a tour of the ship. The sailor announced in broken English that his name was Mr. Na. As Big Guy walked past the galley, he could smell the aroma of Kim Chee, peppers and other exotic food being prepared. Through a maze of narrow hallways and down several worn stairways they walked, until they were down in the engine room, observing the generators and other equipment that kept the ship functioning. The smell of diesel fuel and lubricating oil permeated the air as Mr. Na showed them the engines that hummed in the heart of the ship. After seeing the anchor and the bridge, Mr. Na escorted Big Guy and Johnny to his cabin where they sat on his bunk.

Mr. Na tried hard, in broken English, to explain himself and strike up a conversation. He had hoped to practice his English and learn more about life in the United States. He showed Big Guy and Johnny pictures of his family. After carefully inspecting a handful of pictures, featuring a smiling woman and a child Big Guy handed the pictures to Johnny.

"I understand that education is compulsory in America?" Mr. Na asked.

Big Guy looked to Johnny for the answer, but Johnny was too busy looking at the pictures to notice the urgent question in Big Guy's face.

Finally Big Guy blurted out, "Yes it is! We are required to go to school and everyone pays for it in their taxes."

"Hum", Mr. Na replied as he shook his head to acknowledge his understanding.

"Do you attend school?" Big Guy asked. "No- I sail the ocean. But I would like to continue my school." Mr. Na replied as he looked with longing out at the blue sky that was shining outside the small porthole window, which served as his only source of natural light.

"What do you do on the ship?" Johnny asked after he handed the photos back to Mr. Na.

Mr. Na thought for a moment, as he allowed his brain to translate the proper words from his native tongue into English. "I work in the engine room. I am what you call the ships engineer," Mr. Na finally replied.

"You are like Scotty on the Starship Enterprise!" Johnny exclaimed.

Mr. Na looked puzzled, as Big Guy looked at Johnny and rolled his eyes.

"Never mind him- he watches too much TV," Big Guy replied.

Mr. Na lit up a cigarette and offered it to the boys.

"No thanks, were trying to quit," Big Guy said with a smile.

After exchanging addresses, Mr. Na escorted Big Guy and Johnny to the gangway steps and they bid each other good-bye.

Both of the boys rode away, exhilarated by the experience. By the time, Big Guy pedaled his bicycle into the driveway of his house it was starting to get dark. As Big Guy entered the house, his mother was waiting in the kitchen.

"Where have you been?" Priscilla asked.

"We were riding our bicycles." Big Guy replied.

"And where did you ride your bicycle?" Priscilla asked.

Big Guy paused before answering; his mother knew that she might not want to know the answer to the question.

"We rode our bikes down to the harbor," Big Guy said.

"And where did you go in the harbor?" His mother inquired.

Big Guy sensed that his mother had found out about his big adventure from Johnny's mother. It was a fact that in a close-knit neighborhood like the one Big Guy grew up in; everyone looked out for everyone else. It would be the neighborhood concern that Big Guy might be leading his friend into trouble.

"We went and looked at a ship." Big Guy answered.

"I heard that you actually went aboard a ship down there." Priscilla replied.

"Yes we did, it was really neat! It was a Korean ship and we met a Korean sailor named Mr. Na. You would really like him he is a nice person. He gave me his address so that we can write to each other."

"You be careful down there I don't want you getting shanghaied." Priscilla said half-jokingly.

As Big Guy went to his room, he thought about his adventure that day. "It was like going to Korea!" he thought to himself. "I would like to go to Korea someday".

On the next weekend Big Guy was down in the harbor once again, this time with another friend named Jim. Once again, they stood on the dock staring up at a rusty freighter; this one came from the Soviet Union. Soon enough an officer on board the freighter motioned for the boys to board the ship. As with the Korean ship, after they cleared the gangway, the officer shook their hands and welcomed them in broken English aboard the Freighter *Gamzat Tasadasa*. The officer was a young looking man, who appeared to be in his early thirties, with light blue eyes and short blond hair. He wore a maritime uniform with gold epaulets that included 3 stripes. Again, the usual tour commenced, starting with the engine room where Big Guy and Jim met an older man with salt and pepper colored hair. He was wearing blue overalls covered with grease; and was standing by an electrical panel in knee high rubber boots.

Big Guy sensing that introductions were in order, motioned to him and said, "My name is Mike". He then motioned to the man and asked, "Your name?" The officer spoke to the man in Russian as if to interpret. With a big smile that radiated from under a big bushy mustache the man answered, "Alexi!"

Then Alexi motioned for the group to follow him on a tour of the engine room. As they passed by the engines Alexi smiled and gestured toward the smoothly running rocker arms that lined the large diesel engines. The engines purred as Alexi proudly exhibited his domain to Big Guy and his friend. It was plain to see that while the Freighter may have belonged to the people of the Soviet Union, the engine room belonged to Alexi.

After they left the engine room they walked down a hallway toward the first mate's quarters. Along the way, they passed portraits of Lenin and a Cossack whose name the ship honored. It was like "being in the Soviet Union without leaving home," Big Guy thought as they walked into the first mates quarters.

Once inside the relatively spacious quarters, Big Guy scanned the various pictures of family members that hung on the walls. They were posing in formal clothes, each smiling face lit up by warm sunlight. On one wall hung numerous certificates printed in the Cyrillic alphabet. It was as exotic as Big Guy could imagine as the first officer offered them each a seat and a chocolate bar.

Big Guy readily accepted the candy as the conversation turned to the object that was sitting on the first officer's desk. "Can you help me with something please?" the first mate asked somewhat haltingly.

"Here we go," thought Big Guy, "This guy is some sort of Russian secret agent and he is looking for a double agent to spy for the bad guys. Mom is right we will probably get shanghaied and sent to Siberia", Big Guy thought as the first officer placed a black briefcase in front of them on the desk.

The first officer opened the briefcase to reveal a compact radio with a cassette tape player built into it. Big Guy noticed that the briefcase, made by Panasonic and acquired by the first officer in Japan, was probably a souvenir from the ship's last port of call in Yokohama.

As the first officer pulled up on a telescoping antennae in the briefcase he then asked, "Can you tell me please, what is a good rock and roll station?" To this Big Guy smiled as he showed the first officer where on the dial to find the station.

Big Guy replied, "Of course- that would be rockin FM Stereo KLOS. Soon the sound of Led Zeppelin was pulsing out of the first mates quarters past the watchful gaze of Comrade Lenin.

It was past dinnertime when Big Guy arrived home to face the scorn of his mother.

"You have been down in the harbor again- haven't you?" Priscilla asked.

"Sorry I got home late mom." Big Guy replied.

"I don't want you down in that harbor!" Priscilla protested, her voice ringing loud in Big Guy's ears.

"But mom we went aboard a Russian Ship this time!" Big Guy exclaimed excitedly.

"You went aboard a Russian ship!" Priscilla shrieked. "Now I have to worry about you getting kidnapped by Communists! What are the neighbors going to say when their kids end up with you in prison in Siberia?"

"I hope they packed a warm coat?" Big Guy replied as he tried to get on his mother's better side.

Priscilla smiled reluctantly as Big Guy made a beeline for the stove to dish up his dinner, which consisted of beef stew and biscuits.

"You are something else young man- what am I going to do with you!" Priscilla said with a smile. Big Guy hugged his mother as he sat down to eat.

Devereaux was also spending a great deal of time down in the harbor as a maintenance electrician for a major oil company. He was working nights down in the harbor, maintaining pumping stations. One day Devereaux, knowing that Big Guy wanted to go back to the harbor, offered to take him to work that evening. Big Guy excitedly accepted and both were soon off to Devereaux's workplace. When they arrived, Devereaux showed Big Guy his work truck that he used to inspect the oil pumping stations that were scattered all over this part of the waterfront.

Devereaux's truck was a battered relic that had multicolored fenders and a toolbox in the back.

As the night wore on, Devereaux and Big Guy patrolled the pumping stations, which consisted of large, drab green metal boxes that stood next to grated access pits. The green boxes housed the pumping controls for each oil well, and included one green light and a red light, which was only illuminated if there was a problem with the pumping controls. The pits included a metal ladder that descended into a dark and greasy cellar that was lined with pipes. Devereaux's job was to search for red lights on top of the metal boxes that indicated problems in the system that required the attention of an electrician. As they drove along Devereaux explained the layout of the oilfield and the purpose of each piece of equipment that they drove past. Soon they came across a pumping station with a red light showing. Devereaux and Big Guy walked over to the pumping station as Devereaux opened the panel and proceeded to troubleshoot the electrical system. Before restarting the pumping station, Devereaux lead Big Guy down into the pit below ground that housed a series of pipes and valves. At the end of a small pipe was a spigot that Devereaux opened to show Big Guy the crude oil that was being pumped from deep within the earth. Big Guy tried to touch the viscous liquid, but it was too hot to touch as it flowed from the spigot.

It was midnight, the tide was receding out of the harbor and the waterfront was quiet. Big

Guy had an idea as he sat in Devereaux's work shack. Big Guy proceeded to write a note. It was written to no one in particular. In the note, Big Guy wrote; *"If anyone should find this note, please return it to the following address..."* After Big Guy penned his address, he turned and asked Devereaux if he had a bottle handy.

Soon Big Guy found a bottle with a screw top, placed his note in the bottle, and sealed it up tight. Big Guy wandered to the edge of the sea and tossed the bottle as far as he could into the harbor. He watched as the bottle drifted with the tide out into the darkness.

"It was indeed a big world with many possibilities", thought Big Guy as he drove home with his father that night. When Devereaux and Big Guy got home, Big Guy brushed his teeth and jumped into bed.

That night he fell asleep watching the silhouettes of the gold fish that were swimming lazily in the fish bowl next to his bed. It seemed that life could never be taken for granted in a world where change is the only given and stability more fleeting than we could ever imagine.

The next day was February 9, 1971. Big Guy would be twelve years old in November. It was 6:00 AM when Big Guy was jolted awake by an earthquake that was larger than any earthquake that he had ever experienced. The water in the fish bowl sloshed violently as Big Guy clutched the edges of his bed as it slid around the floor. The initial shock wave was followed by several sharp jolts that felt as though each violent tremor would tear the walls of the house apart. It was then that Big Guy became frightened and started to pray as he leaped from his bed and ran to a doorway to find something solid to hold onto. It was the most helpless that he had ever felt, as the earth under Southern California rang like a bell. The earthquake lasted approximately 60 seconds and registered a magnitude of 6.6.

As the initial shock waves started to subside, Big Guy could feel the earth quiver as if it were not yet finished proclaiming who was ultimately in charge of our lives. Big Guy wandered down the hall to find surprisingly little damage, with only some crooked pictures on the walls. Big Guy soon found Devereaux in the kitchen, cooking up some oatmeal mush for breakfast.

"That was a good one!" Devereaux exclaimed as if earthquakes were a given in his life.

"Was that as bad as the one in 1933?" Big Guy asked.

"No- that was just practice compared to '33", Devereaux replied.

Priscilla wandered into the living room and turned on the TV to find the channels all buzzing with news and rumors about the quake. It was not long before the extent of the quake was known, when the aftershocks started to arrive. As the house started to quiver and the quiver turned to shaking, Priscilla started to pray and Devereaux continued to serve up the mush as though the earthquake was merely an annoyance.

Over the next several weeks, the aftershocks started to subside and life returned to its monotonous regularity for Devereaux and Big Guy.

One night Big Guy found Devereaux sitting in his favorite spot on the steps of the front porch.

"How's my Big Guy doing?" Devereaux asked.

"I'm fine dad." Big Guy replied.

Devereaux continued, "I had a discussion with Howdy Cutter today and I almost had to give him a mental enema."

Howdy, Cutter was a neighbor who lived across the street and served as Devereaux's source of gossip in the neighborhood.

"What did Howdy have to say?" Big Guy asked.

Devereaux replied, "Howdy asked me why you were always hanging around with that retarded kid."

"Was he talking about my friend Greg?" Big Guy asked.

"That's who he was talking about. I told him that I would rather have you hanging around a retarded kid than some dope addict." Devereaux replied.

"Greg doesn't cause any trouble and besides he knows a lot about a lot of things." Big Guy replied.

Big Guy looked up to the dark sky and asked, "I wonder what Larry is doing right now?"

Devereaux smiled, put his arm around Big Guy and replied, "He's smiling down on us with Grandpa Snazzy."

Then Devereaux asked, "How would you like to go up in an airplane next weekend Big Guy?"

"Go up in an airplane!?" Big Guy jumped to his feet. "That would be great! When are we going? Where are we going to fly to?"

Devereaux replied, "I have taken all your brothers up in an airplane, it's time that you went up as well. We will go to Lake Elsinore, there's a place there where skydivers go up to jump."

"Will I get to jump out of an airplane?" Big Guy asked excitedly.

"No your mom would kill me if I let you jump out of an airplane, besides I think that you have to be a bit older before you can jump."

Early that Saturday morning Big Guy was awaken before day break by the booming voice of Devereaux saying, "Time to get up Piggies- we are going flying today!"

Big Guy was up and rubbing his eyes as he struggled to put his jeans on. Soon he wandered into the kitchen to find Devereaux and Priscilla drinking coffee. Big Guy located the cold cereal and still heavy with sleep, he poured some milk into the bowl and proceeded to gaze at the cereal box as he stuffed his mouth with Rice Chex.

"What's it like to fly dad?" Big Guy asked.

"It's hard to explain", Devereaux replied. "It's like being a bird and seeing the world from a different point of view."

"When did you first fly dad?" Big Guy asked as he stuffed another spoonful of cereal into his mouth.

"I had a friend that I went to high school with named Everett who learned to fly at a young age.

Everett and I would rent a plane every so often on the weekends and go flying. He was a good pilot and a very good friend. He introduced me to the pilots at Lake Elsinore and I have gone flying there every so often. Now it's your turn." Devereaux said with a smile.

When it was time to go Priscilla gave Devereaux and Big Guy a hug and gave them her usual blessing, "May God bless and keep you and bring you home safe to me please!"

It was like a rite of passage as Devereaux and Big Guy jumped into the yellow Ford Pickup truck that Devereaux had just purchased used from the local classified ads.

"What do you think of Ol Yeller?" Devereaux asked referring to the pickup truck.

"It's great. It seems to have a lot more power than the old VW Camper Bus." Big Guy remarked as he studied the instrument panel and dashboard.

Pickup trucks were that most American form of transportation, especially in the West, where distance and the need to haul something other than people was always a requirement. Pickup trucks could serve as a place to sleep, or a way to access remote country over bad roads. They were as much a part of the western landscape as the horse and wagon were before them.

By the time Devereaux and Big Guy had arrived at the airport at Lake Elsinore, the hangars were bustling with skydivers and their gear.

Devereaux walked up to the receptionist desk and asked if there was an available flight so that his son could go flying for the first time. The receptionist smiled and walked back to the pilots lounge. Soon an older, grey haired man came to the desk and asked if anyone wanted to go for an airplane ride. Big Guy approached the desk and excitedly replied, "I want to go flying today!"

"Then follow me young man." The pilot said with a smile, as he gave Devereaux a wink. Big Guy followed the pilot and glancing back, saw Devereaux smiling proudly as he waved encouragement to his son.

Big Guy followed the pilot into a large hangar where there were long wooden tables that were used for packing parachutes. Soon they were joined by a jumpmaster who introduced himself to Big Guy as he placed a parachute onto Big Guys back.

"How does that feel?" The jumpmaster asked with a smile.

"That feels pretty good." Big Guy replied, somewhat uncertain as to why he was being fitted for a parachute.

The pilot could see that Big Guy had some concerns regarding the parachute. He smiled as he explained, "The jumpmaster here will explain how to use the parachute in case something goes wrong with the aircraft."

"So I'm not going to have to jump?" Big Guy asked.

"Not unless I tell you to jump, and if that happens you will probably know that something is wrong with the airplane." The pilot continued.

The jumpmaster proceeded to explain the principles of using a parachute, "Once the pilot tells you to jump, position yourself in the door of the aircraft. Then step out of the aircraft in a crouched position and wait until you clear the aircraft. Then pull your ripcord handle to your knees. Stare out at the horizon until you get within a hundred feet or so to the ground. Bend your knees and when you hit the ground -roll."

After the briefing, Big Guy followed the pilot out to an aircraft that was sitting on the tarmac. It was a Howard, a single engine aircraft, which was well suited for skydiving as it had plenty of interior space and in this case a removable door which provided for an oversized exit. Before Big Guy knew it, five parachutists joined them on the flight. Big Guy peered into the interior of the old Howard, to find one pilot seat and one small metal seat facing toward the tail next to the pilot's seat and the large opening where the door should have been. The smaller seat was sloped towards the gaping door to facilitate the egress of parachutists from the aircraft. Behind the seats, there was only a plywood floor and vacant space to allow the skydivers to arrange themselves prior to jumping. One of the jumpers had a camera and explained to Big Guy that he would be filming the jump. He said that he would wave to Big Guy as he jumped. The jumpers loaded into the aircraft first, leaving the sloping seat next to the pilot and the open door to Big Guy.

After all were loaded into the airplane, the pilot started the big engine and after getting the "thumbs up" from all his passengers, he throttled the engine and taxied out onto the runway. Big Guy adjusted his seat belt tighter as he peered out the gaping door next to him. He focused on the tire and the runway as the pilot rolled into position for takeoff. The pilot pulled the throttle back and the old Howard began to respond with a loud roar. Big Guy watched as the runway began to move faster and faster under the tire until the tire lifted off from the earth and gradually slowed its rotation. Big Guy was flying!

He watched as the earth and everything on it became smaller. As he felt the wind blowing through the open door, Big Guy searched the horizon as the mountains spread out in all directions. Thin streams of clouds wisped by as the Howard turned gradual circles to gain altitude, until it was at the proper altitude for skydiving. Big Guy's eyes were glued to every little detail outside the open doorway. Highways became thin grey lines, as rows of green avocado and citrus groves blended with dry rocky creek beds and jagged granite ridges to form the tapestry of native California. The world was even bigger than Big Guy could ever imagine. By experiencing the joy of flight, Big Guy was encouraged to pursue a larger life. While back on the ground, Devereaux could only watch the ascending flight of his son with joy and the knowledge that he was progressing toward manhood.

Soon it was time for the parachutists to jump.

One by one they approached the open door. Then each leaned forward as they dropped out into space, releasing their hold on the world to embrace only the wind. The parachutist with the camera was the last one to the door, as he leaned forward and dropped from the Howard, he looked back and waved at Big Guy as he fell away into the gusting space below.

"Wow- that was neat!" Big Guy thought as he waved back at the falling parachutists.

As the Howard lumbered back to the airport and touched down on the runway, Big Guy was elated with his first experience with flight. As the plane rolled to a stop and the pilot shut down the engine, Big Guy jumped out and met Devereaux standing next to the hanger door. They hugged each other as the pilot walked up and congratulated Big Guy for his accomplishment.

As Devereaux and Big Guy drove along Ortega Highway toward the setting sun, Big Guy fell asleep watching the shadows dance in the trees along the road. It was a day that would live in his memory for the rest of his life.

****

Several months later Devereaux mentioned to Big Guy that he had purchased a metal building "for cheap" from a junk dealer who had purchased it from an oil company over by Signal Hill. Big Guy jumped into the VW Bug with Devereaux and off they went to check it out. After driving by countless pump jacks in an oil field, they turned into a dusty vacant lot covered with tumbleweeds and there standing decrepit and abandoned was a corrugated metal building that had served as a tool shed for many years.

"That's it?" Big Guy asked.

"I got that for $200.00- can you imagine that?" Devereaux replied with a smile.

"It doesn't even have any windows." Big Guy said as he smiled at his dad.

"How are you going to get that up north?" Big Guy asked.

"I'm working on that," Devereaux replied.

Within a week Devereaux had rented a utility trailer and with a little help from Sheila's husband Bob, they had dismantled the shed and loaded it onto the trailer. Big Guy didn't accompany his dad on this trip, the space was necessary for carrying tools, extra beer and Bob. The story goes that the two completed the assembly in two days with only a few conflicts of opinion and a case of beer between them. Big Guy didn't see the finished product until that fall.

A month later, Devereaux drove up to the house in a one ton, 1950 flatbed Chevy truck. Devereaux had bought it for $500.00 from an old man in Orange County.

"Wow what's the truck for dad?" Big Guy asked as he ran up to the driver's side door.

"I figured that if we are going to move stuff into the shack on the Sheep Ranch, we will need a truck to haul it." Devereaux replied.

In a week the first hauling mission began. Much to Big Guy's surprise, Devereaux's plan was to leave the old truck up on the Sheep

Ranch. In order to pull that off, Devereaux took the old truck over to a loading dock by the railroad tracks while Brian and Big Guy followed in the VW Bug. Within no time Devereaux had the VW Bug loaded onto the flatbed, along with old ladders and other odds and ends.

Perhaps he was reliving the Dust Bowl days, Big Guy could not quite understand Devereaux's logic, but by 6 o'clock in the morning the next day, the two intrepid travelers were on the road again, struggling to keep the speedometer at 40 MPH going over the Grapevine toward Bakersfield. It's funny how history repeats itself and refugees march across the pages of time.

"What's a Southern Californian's third word dad?" Big Guy asked his father as the old truck was passed by everything on the freeway.

"It's momma, papa and Wenatchee. That's what it is!" Big Guy laughed as the old truck rumbled into Bakersfield.

It took two days to make it to the town of Weed, in northern California where Devereaux noticed a large bulge in the sidewall of the right-front tire.

"Oh Shit!" Devereaux exclaimed as he began to get irritated by the sight of the damaged tire.

"What's wrong?" Big Guy asked.

"We are about to lose a tire." Devereaux replied.

"I thought that the engine would blow before we needed a new tire." Big Guy continued.

Devereaux had been dumping a quart of oil in the old truck every 150 miles.

"Hopefully we can make it to Klamath Falls. We will get a motel and cross that bridge in the morning." Devereaux said as he jumped back into the driver's seat.

They spent that night in an old motel in Weed, where they watched a grainy picture on TV of an old western from the 1930s.

"I haven't seen that movie since I was a kid back in 1934. That actor has been dead for a while." Devereaux said as he sipped a beer and took a bite from a polish sausage that he had bought at the local Safeway.

"Did I ever tell you that your grandpa use to play any musical instrument that had strings?" Devereaux asked with a smile.

"I think that you told me that he played the fiddle." Big Guy replied.

"He played anything with strings, including the mandolin and the guitar. Some nights he would sit in the living room with the radio turned off and just sing and play. He liked old cowboy songs from the late 1800s. His favorite was *Buffalo Girl*- Oh buffalo girl won't you come out tonight, come out tonight, come out tonight..." Devereaux smiled and sang as his mind slipped back into that simple, sweet melody and he thought about how much he loved his father.

Big Guy stared at his father for a while as silence filled the room.

"You miss your dad don't you?" Big Guy asked.

"He was such a great guy; you will never have the dad that I did." Devereaux replied as tears welled up in his eyes.

"I would have loved to hear him play." Big Guy replied.

"He didn't know how to read music; he just played songs by ear." Devereaux continued.

"I still think that MY dad is the best dad ever!" Big Guy said with a smile.

The next day after eating breakfast at McDonalds, the two of them slowly drove 70 miles from Weed and rolled into Klamath Falls around lunch time. On the right was a large lumber mill, complete with a wigwam burner that spewed fragrant blue smoke across the valley. Devereaux pulled into the mill and immediately looked for the nearest loading dock. Just then a young mill worker approached and asked if he could help. Big Guy was shocked when Devereaux asked the mill worker how he would like to have an old, 2 ton truck?

"For nothing?" the mill worker replied excitedly.

"Just show me where your loading dock is so that I can unload this car and it's yours," Devereaux replied.

Within 15 minutes the Volkswagen was unloaded and stuffed to the brim with ice chests and much of the load that was on the back of the old truck. Devereaux signed the title to the truck on the spot, as the mill worker danced around like he had won the lottery.

"You might need a new tire and it burns a little oil," Devereaux volunteered as he handed the title to the new owner.

It was almost dark when they stopped alongside of the Klickitat River in southern Washington and fell sound asleep in their seats.

The next day around noon they arrived at the Sheep Ranch. There standing in the sagebrush on a small rise was the corrugated metal shed standing in all its rusted glory. Big Guy got out of the Volkswagen and wandered over to the door of the shed.

"Watch out for rattlesnakes," Devereaux said as Big Guy opened the door and peeked inside. The shed was dark inside, except for the small beams of concentrated sunlight that poured in through a multitude of nail holes. The floor was dirt and the walls had nails from which dangled all sorts of junk: from worn out work boots to canvas water bags to an old Coleman gas cook stove. That night after the campfire died out, Big Guy slept in the car seat, while Devereaux slept in the tool shed.

Chapter 7

Face to Face With Eternity

One day in 1973, when Big Guy was thirteen years old, his mother brought him to the doctor's for a routine physical so that he could play junior high school football. After the nurse had taken his blood pressure, she looked puzzled and took it again. The doctor soon came into the room and repeated the blood pressure exam. Upon seeing Big Guy's blood pressure, the doctor proceeded to check it once again. After the second test, the doctor mentioned that Big Guy's blood pressure was elevated. The doctor ordered a blood test and a urine test. Having completed the tests, Priscilla drove Big Guy back home. On the way, Big Guy noticed that his mother had a look of concern on her face.

"Don't worry mom I'm just fine," Big Guy said with a smile.

"I've been through this before; I don't need to experience this again." Priscilla replied.

Within a week, Big Guy was back in the hospital undergoing more tests. Because of his brother's death from cancer, several doctors who were concerned with some of the results of his medical tests were scrutinizing Big Guy's health. It was at this time that Big Guy started to fear those trips to the hospital. He remembered clearly the suffering that Larry had endured and feared that he too would be confined to a room without a window. Could it be that he had the same cancer growing in him? To Big Guy it would be a death sentence.

As the sun set behind clouds of car exhaust and the emissions of the oil refineries, Big Guy wondered if he would ever see another sort of life in which the sky was clear and the future bright.

Some time had passed when the doctors suggested a strange follow-up with regard to Big Guy's case. They asked that the whole family submit to a urine test. This request did not go over too well with Devereaux; it was one thing to be poking and prodding one of his sons and quite another to intrude on the rest of the family in such a manner. But in the end the doctors won out and after studying the inner workings of the family concluded that Big Guy's unusual test results were merely genetic anomalies that were unworthy of any further study.

This temporary, yet frightening episode in Big Guy's life had ended. But it was an episode that reminded Big Guy of the fragility of life. "There was far too much left to see and do in my life," Big Guy thought. It was time for him to hit the road again.

It was June of 1973, Devereaux and Big Guy were on the road once again; this time the destination was Glacier and Yellowstone National Parks. As usual, the trip included a stop at the Sheep Ranch. While there, Devereaux and Big Guy stopped in at the museum in Waterville, Washington. Inside the museum, they viewed many varieties of farm implements and old photos as well as a taxidermy calf with two heads.

That night the two gathered by the campfire after dinner and pondered the stars above. As they gazed into the immense darkness, a shooting star streaked across the northern sky. While Devereaux and Big Guy might have been separated by a generation, they were now joined by many common experiences and a deeper kinship stirred their relationship.

"I remember when I was young and your grandmother Lefty had me working when I was eight years old. I spent many hours down at the beach renting umbrellas and selling *Liberty Magazines*. Your old dad always had a little bit of dinero because I always worked. It wasn't a bad life, I had a good childhood." Devereaux gazed out into the darkness as the coyotes howled in the distance.

"What was your favorite memory of growing up back then dad," Big Guy asked.

"I think that my favorite memory was being with my family around the dinner table. Many people did not have enough to eat and yet there we were- well fed, wearing decent clothes and all of us together in one place. Grandpa Snazzy had a good job during the depression. He worked for the city as an electrical inspector. It was his job to inspect the wiring in people's houses and businesses. You would be amazed by the electrical work that he would find back then. People were always trying to find a way to bypass the meters in their houses, so that they would not have to pay for electricity. This resulted in some pretty Oklahoma wiring jobs. Your granddad actually carried a gun, because some of the locations and situations that he found himself in were kind of dangerous." Devereaux replied as his dark eyes gazed into the glowing coals of the fire.

Just then, another shooting star streaked across the sky.

Devereaux exclaimed, "Did you see that beautiful shooting star? That reminds me of the stories that my parents told me about the arrival of Haley's comet back in 1910. They were both living in the Arizona Territory back then, so the sky was clear most of the time. Old Grandpa Snazzy had a little Brownie Camera that he took pictures with and one night he actually captured a photo of the comet."

"I would sure like to see that!" Big Guy exclaimed, his face bathed in the orange fire light.

"Remind me and I will show that picture to you Big Guy," Devereaux replied with a smile.

Devereaux had purchased a camper for the pickup truck before they had left on this trip. As usual, a certain amount of improvisation had to take place in order to accommodate the used camper. Devereaux had left the tailgate on the truck and this required that the tailgate be lowered in order to open the door to the camper. The camper was two feet higher than the cab of the pickup. This allowed for a certain amount of headroom as one entered it. Once inside one found two plywood boards attached by hinges to the sidewalls of the camper. Attached to the boards were two by fours, also attached by hinges, to the plywood. So if one wanted to sleep in the back of the camper all they had to do was flip a hook to release the plywood down to a level position supported by the two by fours. In addition to a larger window in the rear door and another window in the front, on each side of the camper was located one small window.

After dousing the campfire, Devereaux and Big Guy jumped into the camper and rolled out their sleeping bags on the plywood bunks.

As Big Guy pulled the sleeping bag up around his nose, he fell asleep listening to the lonely howls of nearby coyotes, as thoughts of Haley's Comet filtered through his mind and the planet earth continued on its path through the universe.

The next day they departed the Sheep Ranch early in the morning and were soon driving through the wheat fields of Eastern Washington on U.S. Highway 2. The green fields passed by in an endless procession and Big Guy was mesmerized by their symmetry and scale.

After filling up with gas and acquiring some food, Devereaux and Big Guy headed towards Northern Idaho. It was late afternoon when they found Springy Point Campground on the banks of Lake Pend Oreille. Before long camp was set up and it was time to go swimming. With Devereaux in his massive blue swimming shorts and Big Guy in a pair of cut off Levi's, the two wandered down to the lake and jumped in the cool water. As Devereaux bobbed around in the water, Big Guy swam over to a floating dock and climbed aboard. As a large osprey circled overhead, Devereaux turned onto his back like some sort of walrus and paddled in circles until he too was at the floating dock. Big Guy moved over and Devereaux climbed up and sat next to him. "Look at that big eagle up there," Devereaux, said.

Big Guy looked up just in time to see the osprey dive to the lake and snatch a large fish in its talons.

"Wow did you see that dad?" Big Guy asked excitedly.

"Did I ever tell you about the time when I was having lunch on the offshore oil platform?" Devereaux asked.

"I was sitting by the edge of the platform watching some pigeons peck around by some pilings at the water's edge. As I was watching, suddenly there was a commotion and one of the pigeons was pulled under the water by a crab. You don't see that every day." Devereaux said as he gazed at the blue sky above.

That night around the campfire Devereaux and Big Guy talked about everything from politics to religion. Not far from their campsite, a train trestle spanned one of the many bays along the lake. Soon they heard the lonely sound of a train horn approaching from the north. Before long, a Great Northern freight train rumbled past on its way south. In the dim light Big Guy could see rail cars full of finished wood passing by in the night.

"Did you know that your great grandfather was a section foreman for a railroad in Eastern Oregon?" Devereaux asked.

"No I didn't know that." Big Guy replied. "Your Great Grandfather William Orpheus worked on the Sumpter Valley Railroad; he also worked for the Union Pacific back in the 1890s out of Baker City Oregon.

He lived with the family for a while in a boxcar next to the tracks, along with a large number of Japanese laborers. It was hard, dangerous work back then and he learned to respect those people."

Big Guy replied, "Then you had to fight them in World War II."

Devereaux looked at Big Guy and said, "Even though I spent close to four years in the South Pacific fighting jungle rot and dysentery, I never had anything against the Japanese. We all had to contribute to the war effort and I just did my job. Before the war, some of my friends were Japanese. I noticed that they all worked hard and worked to better themselves and the community. All of them ended up in a camp at Tule Lake, in northern California. They lost everything. I still feel bad about that."

After a long pause, Big Guy soberly asked Devereaux, "Did you ever have to kill any Japanese during the war?"

Devereaux smiled, rolled his eyes and replied, "No I never had to kill anyone. I was on a fleet repair ship called the Ajax- old AR 6. I was a member of the commissioning crew, which means that I was on the first crew that the Ajax ever had after it was built down in Los Angeles Harbor at the start of the war."

Devereaux poked at the campfire with a blackened stick.

"We were a crew of misfits- construction workers mostly, who were more concerned with shore leave and when our next meal would be served, than killing Japanese."

Big Guy looked at Devereaux and smiled as Devereaux continued.

"We fought a different kind of war. We worked on ships that could barely float, because they had been so battered by shelling. It was like attending to the needs of wounded soldiers returning from the battle. The old Ajax could perform most of the repairs that were required while the warships were still at sea. This allowed those warships to get back into action quicker. We could fix anything from radios to torpedoes to navigation systems.

But there were times when even the old Ajax couldn't help.

I remember the time, after the carrier USS Franklin had been disabled by kamikazes at the Battle of Leyte Gulf; our Captain John Louser

Brown asked the Captain of the Franklin if he required the Ajax's help. The Franklin was barely limping along under its own power; it was listing heavily to one side and partially obscured by smoke from some fires that were still burning under the deck. As it passed by the Ajax, we watched as it continued on-heading back to San Francisco like some beat up prize fighter.

Toward the end of the war we had an outbreak of dysentery that ended up killing some of our crew mates including one guy in the bunk above me."

Devereaux stared into the campfire as he said,

"They were the greatest bunch of guys that you could ever work with. Yep- it was the greatest navy ever assembled in one place. I saw it with my own eyes the day that I climbed up to fix the anemometer way up on the highest mast of the ol Jax. When I was up there the fleet was assembled for the final invasion of Japan. I looked out over the whole 7th Fleet- battleship after battleship, cruiser after cruiser, aircraft carrier after aircraft carrier. All the support ships extending over the horizon as far as my eyes could see. At that moment I knew that I was witnessing history and that the world would never see a sight like that ever again."

Tears came to Devereaux's eyes as the firelight danced across his weathered face.

"I remember those dark nights out on the fantail of the ship, in the middle of the South Pacific so far from home. The ocean was like a dark canvas and the sky was a mass of stars. On some nights the whole ocean was fluorescent blue from the luminescence of countless sea creatures below us. The propellers of the ships churned a blue wake for miles."

They talked late into the night as the lights of Sandpoint sparkled on the surface of Lake Pond Oreille.

The next day they were heading east on US Highway 2 toward Libby, Montana. The forested mountains flew by, as they crossed several bridges that spanned rushing streams of cold, crystalline water.

Soon they entered the town of Kalispell where they stopped for groceries and a half case of Lucky Lager.

After filling up with gasoline they pointed Ol Yeller east and headed toward Glacier National Park, passing through Columbia Falls and finally into the Park at West Glacier.

At the entrance station, Big Guy stared mesmerized at the National Park Ranger, who was dressed in his official uniform that included a straw ranger hat. Devereaux paid the entrance fee and the ranger handed Devereaux a map and other information, as they entered the park. The ranger seemed happy in his work as he smiled at Big Guy in the passenger seat.

The northern Rocky Mountains rose toward the clear sky above them. Deep forests of fir and Lodgepole Pine lined the highway ahead, as the smell of sun drenched pine resin filled the air.

"Could you imagine making a living working in a place like this?" Big Guy said as he surveyed the landscape that unfolded before them.

"Your old dad could never make a living in a place like this." Devereaux replied.

"That's too bad." Big Guy said. "I'm tired of living in LA County." he continued.

"It has always been good to me. I could always make a living there" Devereaux replied.

"I think that it's a shithole." Big Guy replied. "That shithole kept my family fed-including you." Devereaux replied somewhat irritated that Big Guy would question his father's choice of life paths.

"I know that you had to keep us fed dad, but it's still a shithole and I don't want to have to depend upon that place for a living." Big Guy said.

The landscape opened up as Lake McDonald appeared on the left and continued for as far as the eye could see until the highway started to wind higher into the mountains.

Higher they drove, past plunging waterfalls and high elevation ice fields where a highway should not be. When they reached Logan Pass, they stopped at a Visitor Center to take in the unbelievable beauty of the landscape around them.

Devereaux walked to the viewpoint and gazed out over mountains and snowfields that spread out in all directions. Big Guy followed as they paused to take in as much of the moment as they could. Before them was Hidden Lake. The lake was as still as glass and the reflection of several prominent peaks rose from the still water into the clear sky. The peaks were rocky, snow covered and wild, with no sign of any human presence. Ragged stringers of wind blasted trees lined long avalanche scutes that ran clear to the edge of the lake.

Big Guy said, "Could you imagine making a living working in a place like this?"

They continued their journey along the Going to the Sun Highway until they found themselves at a rest area north of Depuyer, Montana. It was dark when they arrived and a cold wind blew off the east slopes of the Rockies.

Devereaux and Big Guy clamored into the camper and were soon sound asleep to the sound of the wind as it jostled the camper from side to side, as if to the rhythm of a gentle lullaby.

The next morning found them sitting on the tailgate, bowls of cereal in hand, as Devereaux was explaining to Big Guy the difference between an automatic and a manual transmission.

"A manual transmission will save you some gasoline over time." Devereaux said.

"But what do you think about the cost of an automatic transmission up front?" Big Guy replied.

"That's a good point." Devereaux replied.

A soaring hawk caught their attention and the conversation faded. It was the first time that Big Guy had ever been east of the Rocky Mountains. He was astounded to see such high plains.

"The sky is close enough to touch," Big Guy thought as the rolling grasslands hurried by. Big Guy sensed that he had traded the geologic world of the Pacific Coast for the sky-dominated world of the Great Plains.

Somehow, the big sky was intimidating to Big Guy. Perhaps he had seen the *Wizard of Oz* one too many times and the notion of a vengeful tornado attacking them without warning from a landscape that offered so little shelter had suddenly become all too real.

Wolf Creek and then Butte passed by as Devereaux finally stopped at a gas station just before Bozeman. After wiping the windows, Big Guy jumped back into the cab of the truck as Devereaux paid the attendant and they continued their journey toward Gardiner, Montana.

Not too far from Gardner, they entered the north entrance to Yellowstone National Park. Once again, there was a National Park Ranger to greet them and collect the entrance fee.

Once again, Big Guy said, "Could you imagine making a living working in a place like this?"

The thought of working in the outdoors and living in some obscure town fascinated Big Guy. He began to ponder the possibilities of such a life, starting with the first stop ahead, the Visitor's Center at Mammoth Hot Springs. Big Guy started a conversation with a college aged park ranger about how he got a job there and where he lived.

During this conversation, Big Guy overwhelmed the ranger with questions ranging from education to the application process. Every ranger has had the experience of dealing with the curious and clingy nature lover, bent upon conversation and curious about life in such beautiful places; and this encounter was not going to be any different.

After the conversation in which the ranger did a great job of explaining the employment process, including his own experience with that process, Big Guy wandered back over to where Devereaux was reading an interpretive sign and said, "I think that I could actually do a job like that."

"It gets really cold here in the winter," Devereaux replied.

"Wouldn't it be great to live in a place with snow?" Big Guy continued.

"Not fourteen feet of it!" Devereaux exclaimed.

Big Guy could sense a growing friction between himself and his father on the subject of lifestyles. Some of this friction was generational and much of it involved a certain clash of values.

To Devereaux the choices were clear and straight forward; one's path in life was dictated more by fate and economic necessity, than by any sense of aesthetic beauty or self-determined enlightenment. Devereaux was a man raised by the hardened, rough and tumble fortitude of parents whose lives were forged by a nineteenth century reality, a reality in which life was hard, unforgiving and short. To Devereaux true economic freedom and the beauty of geographic choice was a luxury, reserved only for the gentry' class; it was simply not realistic to expect anything more than rush hour traffic and the confined desperation that Los Angeles represented. For blue collar, working people, the availability of work was the only geography that counted and for Devereaux and many other working people- Los Angeles was the only option.

After two weeks on the road, it was evening when Devereaux and Big Guy drove west over Cajon Pass, to see the lights of Southern California glistening in the distance.

It was midnight and Big Guy was asleep by the time they drove into the driveway of their home on Tulane Avenue in Long Beach.

"It's time to get up Big Guy." Devereaux said as he shook his son's shoulder.

"Where are we dad?" Big Guy replied.

"You're home." Devereaux replied.

"Oh ya- home." Big Guy replied as he wandered into the house and down the hall to his room, where he collapsed onto his bed; all automatic and without hesitation, as if the way to bed had been imprinted on him since the day he was born.

It was the comfortable automation of living one's life in the fashion expected that frightened Big Guy the most. Living in a world without beauty and heart felt deliberation was the Boogie Man that haunted his dreams.

****

Chapter 8

A Family Reconstituted

It was the summer of 1971 and Big Guy's brother Brian was getting married to his high school sweetheart. It had been the fourth marriage to take place within a timespan of three years for the Meehan family. The wedding was a great celebration after some turbulent times that seemed like they would never end.

At this time, Big Guy and his best friend Johnny served as altar boys around the block at Saint Cornelius Catholic Church. They both served as such during the wedding, which allowed Big Guy an opportunity to share in that moment with the last of his brothers. It had only been a few months earlier when Sheila had married Bob the Marine, who she had waited for to return from Vietnam.

At the wedding reception, Big Guy and Johnny discovered the Champagne and it was not very long before each of them was singing and stumbling down the beach.

When Priscilla discovered the condition that they were both in; their party was abruptly ended and both were escorted home unceremoniously.

From that moment on Big Guy had become an only child. The family was gradually healing from the trauma of the 1960's; the death of Priscilla's mother and Larry, the assassinations, the political unrest, the losses of Vietnam, and the general turmoil within the family.

Big Guy's life was still bumping along with the changes that growing older represented. His future seemed bright and it opened before him, like an open highway under a pickup truck with a clean windshield and a full tank of gasoline.

One day after school as Big Guy walked into the house he heard the phone ringing.

"Hello." Big Guy answered.

The voice on the other end asked, "Is Devereaux there?"

Big Guy replied, "No- he's at work right now."

The mysterious voice continued, "Who are you?"

Sensing that this stranger was a friend of Devereaux, Big Guy replied, "I'm his number five son- Cinco."

"Cinco?" the voice replied with a laugh.

"My name is Everett and I'm a friend of your dad. I just landed at the airport and was wondering if you would like to go for a ride in my airplane?" the voice asked.

"Meet me down at the airport by the north taxiway," the voice continued.

"It will take me about a half hour to get there- is that okay?" Big Guy replied excitedly.

"Sure- I can wait," said the voice.

Within a minute Big Guy was on his bicycle and pedaling furiously toward the airport, some three miles distant. Within twenty minutes, Big Guy was approaching the terminal at Long Beach Airport.

There on the north taxiway by the chain link gate was a small Cessna with a smiling pilot at the controls. Big Guy leaned his bike up against the fence and proceeded through the gate. He approached the airplane as the pilot opened the passenger door and motioned for Big Guy to jump in. Big Guy climbed into the airplane as the pilot shook his hand and introduced himself.

"Hello Cinco I'm Everett. Your dad and I grew up together here in Long Beach back when I wasn't so old and ugly."

"Hello Everett!" Big Guy replied as he shook Everett's hand.

Everett was a trim, kindly looking, middle-aged man with slightly graying hair and an easy manner about him. Everett handed Big Guy a set of headphones that were setting on the steering yoke in front of him as he started the engine and started to taxi toward the runway for takeoff.

"We will just take a little spin over town, so you won't be gone for long. Just click on your seatbelt and put on your headphones." Everett said as he contacted the control tower and received clearance for takeoff.

Big Guy could not fathom how Everett could understand any of the instructions streaming over the radio. They were continuous and directed at several aircraft simultaneously, including a Pacific Southwest Airlines jet that was just landing as Everett directed the Cessna toward the runway.

"Just press this button to talk to me and don't press this other button here unless you have something important to tell these other motor mouths on the radio." Everett said as he slowed to a stop just before the runway.

"Long Beach Control this is Cessna 364 requesting permission to depart runway 49 Left." Everett spoke into his mic in a crisp voice.

"Cessna 364 you are clear for 49 Left, precede 349 and hold 3,000 MSL." The tower replied as Everett throttled the Cessna up and rolled down the runway. Big Guy watched each move that Everett made closely, as the Cessna gained speed and soon raised up off the runway.

Everett looked over at Big Guy with a smile, as the Cessna gained elevation over the rooftops and lawns below. Big Guy's hometown unfolded below him until the ocean formed a blue barrier on the west side of the city.

Soon Everett leveled the Cessna, trimmed the wings and the engine and then confirmed his position with the tower.

"So what do you think of this flying business Cinco?" Everett asked Big Guy with a smile.

"This is great!" Big Guy replied.

"How would you like to fly this thing?" Everett continued.

"Can I? I mean is that okay?" Big Guy replied.

"Sure- take a hold of the wheel. Do you see those peddles on the floor?" Everett asked.

"Yes." Big Guy replied.

"Put your feet on those peddles." Everett replied.

Everett continued, "Now those peddles control how you turn this thing along with the steering wheel. Do you notice how you can pull in and out on the steering wheel?"

"Yep." Big Guy replied.

"Now turn the wheel just a little." Everett continued.

Big Guy turned the wheel and the Cessna responded with a yawl to the right and then to the left.

"Now pull on the steering wheel." Everett said with smile.

Big Guy pulled on the steering wheel and the Cessna climbed higher until Everett told Big Guy to level the aircraft back again. As Big Guy pushed in on the yoke, he over compensated for the position of the yoke, sending the Cessna into a shallow dive.

"Whoa there big fella," Everett said as he took control of the yoke and re trimmed the aircraft.

"Sorry about that." Big Guy replied.

"Keep flying Cinco- hold onto that steering wheel." Everett said.

Big Guy once again took control of the aircraft as the homes of thousands of his fellow citizens passed by below, unaware of the training flight taking place three thousand feet above them.

Soon Big Guy was flying straight and level as he began to understand how the aircraft responded to the movement of the controls. After a few minutes of level flight, Everett once again took control of the Cessna and headed back towards the airport.

"Your dad and I use to go flying back when we were just a little older than you." Everett said with a smile. "Those were the days."

Later Big Guy learned that Everett had flown 25 missions over the South Pacific during World War II piloting a dive-bomber; those were indeed "the days."

Soon the wide runway appeared in front of them as Everett lined up and touched down with a slight thump. Everett taxied over to the gate where Big Guy had left his bike.

He stopped where Big Guy had jumped in and as Big Guy took off his headset and unbuckled his seat belt, Everett said,

"Make sure that you tell your dad hello for me and tell him to give me a call when he gets the chance. Take care of yourself Cinco; it was good to meet you. Keep yourself straight and level."

Big Guy jumped out and waved as Everett taxied away. It had been an amazing and unexpected day and he could hardly wait to get home and tell his parents what had happened.

That evening at dinner, Big Guy told the story of his airplane ride to his mom and dad. Devereaux smiled as he thought about his old friend Everett and the times that they had in the early years.

"Everett would do chores down at the Airport and the pilots there taught him how to fly", Devereaux said with a smile.

Devereaux continued, "If he paid for the fuel they would let him fly their airplanes. Many a time we would go flying in an old yellow Stearman Biplane; the kind of airplane like the one they use to crop dust. It was a two seater and old Everett and I would spend the day touring the skies over Southern California.

Every so often Everett would practice some acrobatics like loops and turns. Those were the days", Devereaux said with a smile. I'm glad that you had the chance to meet Everett- he's a swell guy."

Priscilla looked at Big Guy and Devereaux and shook her head,

"That's all I need is for you to go flying with some old man who likes to do loop the loops in old airplanes!"

Devereaux's mother Ethel died in the spring of 1973. She was 87 years old and had been alive when the Wright Brothers first flew at Kitty Hawk and Neil Armstrong first stepped onto the surface of the moon.

Born into humble circumstances in a mining camp within the Superstition Mountains of the Arizona Territory in the last decades of the nineteenth century; she witnessed two World Wars, the advent of the automobile and the admission of the Arizona Territory into the Union as the 48th State.

She had mesmerized Big Guy with her tales of the Wild West, enriching his life as she passed along timeless lessons on the power of ordinary people to overcome adversity.

Devereaux could only listen in silence as the Catholic priest spoke of the faithful woman who had sustained him when his father had died unexpectedly when he was only sixteen.

With the death of Devereaux's mother, another cycle of the generations was completed. The family, once again reminded of the nature of loss, gathered to celebrate another life well lived.

As the summer of 1973 approached, Devereaux had convinced Priscilla that it was time for her to take a trip with him and Big Guy up to God's country. She could see the Sheep Ranch for herself and maybe even take a trip into Canada.

After some weeks of consideration, Priscilla agreed to go and the three of them to hit the road.

The next morning after loading up the camper, Devereaux managed to get Priscilla packed and the three started their journey north.

Two days later, they arrived in Wenatchee, where Priscilla thought that it would be a good idea to stay in a motel for the night. It was a good thing, as the next few days were not going to be to her liking as it turned out.

In the afternoon on the next day, Devereaux drove onto the four acres and turned off the engine. It was summer and the windows were down. The air temperature was warm, as a slight breeze blew into the window of the pickup. As the silence descended upon them, Priscilla looked around and could only smile. Devereaux had owned this property for five years and this was the first time that Priscilla had ever seen it.

"I must say that I'm not surprised", Priscilla said with a smile.

Big guy jumped out of the pickup and started to explore the property, as Devereaux climbed out and stretched his legs.

"Well what do you think Beauteous?" Devereaux asked Priscilla.

"It's nice," Priscilla said as she stared out over the vast sage covered expanse in front of her. Without knowing it, Priscilla shared the feelings of all those pioneer women who had followed their husbands to some lonely place where the notions of women were largely unmapped. As the day proceeded, Priscilla took on the job of preparing dinner- as if she had never left home.

After Priscilla donned Devereaux's old linemen's boots, they spent the next day hiking around the property as Devereaux spoke of developing it; so that in the future they would have a place to stay that was better than a camper.

Big Guy never forgot that day, as he watched his mother walking through the sagebrush steppes of North Central Washington in a pink dress and black work boots.

Big Guy listened to his parents speak that day, as they bantered back and forth to each other; with such familiarity that it almost was as if they had been born twins.

The next day they decided to drive into Canada and do some sightseeing. Strangely enough, Priscilla was still wearing Devereaux's work boots and that pink dress that she had worn the day before.

By the end of the day, they were walking down the streets of Penticton, British Columbia; stopping to peer into the storefronts that lined Main Street.

They stopped in front of a record shop, where Devereaux noticed a display that was advertising Beatles music. As Devereaux stared at the photos of the four English musicians, he began to rant about how much he hated those "Limey Sons of Bitches".

Devereaux, never known for being soft-spoken, made Big Guy think that it would be a good time to go for a walk farther down the street.

Moreover, as Big Guy created some distance between himself and his ranting father, he noticed that his mother resembled a hillbilly in her pink dress and black work boots.

Priscilla was getting irritated by Devereaux's diatribe and started to walk away, leaving Devereaux to carry on his rant alone.

At the time, Devereaux failed to notice that it was just him who was left standing in front of the record store, as a grey haired Canadian gentleman came strolling up behind him.

"Look at those Limey Bastards with their long hair; they all look like they need an enema. The guy's on the old Ajax would have had them for lunch. I bet that their mothers love them...I Wanna Hold Your Hand...what a bunch of assholes!" Devereaux exclaimed, as he looked to where Priscilla was standing only a moment earlier.

The old Canadian gentleman just stood behind Devereaux and quietly watched the mad man who was telling the universe what he really thought of the Beatles.

As Devereaux turned around, he discovered that he had been talking to a passing stranger in a foreign country who probably liked the

Queen and the Beatles. The old Canadian merely tipped his hat and smiled, as he continued on his way, not sure what to make of the agitated American who was yelling at a poster of the Beatles down on Main Street.

Priscilla and Big Guy were cringing as they both tried to hold their laughter.

Soon Devereaux came walking up to them, "Did you see that Canadian, he must not like the Beatles either," he said with a smile.

Priscilla just smiled and replied, "Come on you old goat!"

To which Devereaux replied, "At least my mother still loves me."

They traveled east into Banff National Park in Alberta, taking in Lake Louise and the Canadian Rockies. Priscilla later acknowledged that spectacular jaunt as one of the favorites that she had ever taken with Devereaux.

After spending the night at a motel in Edmonton, they continued farther east along the Yellowhead Highway into Saskatchewan, before turning south toward North Dakota.

By the time they had returned home, Devereaux had accepted that his mother had passed and he himself was growing older.

During this adventure with his parents, Big Guy had begun to notice a pain in his right side that was constant.

Several days passed before Big Guy mentioned it to his mother. When he finally did mention it, Big Guy, doubled over by the pain, was complaining loudly.

Priscilla rushed him to the hospital, where he was admitted for Appendicitis. Lucky for Big Guy he was operated on before his appendix had ruptured.

Big Guy had been seriously impacted by the experience. Since his past experience of being given a possible diagnosis of incurable cancer, Big Guy had learned to hate hospitals. Therefore, it was a God send that all of his brothers and sister came to pay him a visit one evening in the hospital.

They had been through a lot- that family of his. Even though Big Guy was in pain and more than a little "under the weather", his siblings managed to try in every way to make him laugh. That night in spite of being sedated and bound by a tightly stitched wound in his right side, Big Guy could not help laughing until he cried. His family had been reconstituted and the joy of being together soon outweighed the suffering that had pulled them apart.

Chapter 9

The 1970's

In the summer of 1973 Devereaux purchased a used red fiberglass Volkswagen Dune Buggy, with bucket seats and a golf ball on the stick shift.

On weekends Devereaux would take Big Guy to the harbor where he would let him drive the dune buggy over the unpaved lots that would later become the site of one of the largest container loading terminals in the world.

They would visit all their favorite haunts in that vehicle and it proved to be one of Big Guy's favorites. It was the vehicle in which Big Guy learned to drive and to a native Southern Californian, a driver's license was almost as important as life itself.

Devereaux towed the dune buggy north and Big Guy drove it all over the back roads of Douglas County.

Big Guy was thirteen years old that summer and his life stretched out before like a western highway. As the wheat fields waved in the afternoon breeze, a cloud of dust followed him as he traveled these roads less taken and gained confidence in his driving abilities.

One day Big Guy was driving Devereaux back toward the Sheep Ranch, when Devereaux noticed that Big Guy was not slowing down for a barb wire gate that was closed ahead.

"You do see that fence don't you?" Devereaux urgently asked.

As Big Guy was about to ask, "What Fence?" he jammed on the brakes and skidded to a stop.

Devereaux replied, "The fence that you almost drove through! Here let me drive until you get your eyes checked." Devereaux said as he switched seats with Big Guy. Big Guy has worn glasses ever since.

In 1974 the first energy crisis hit Southern California with a jolt, as lines formed at the pump and gasoline prices hit 75 cents a gallon.

One day in January Big Guy was in the pickup with Devereaux waiting in line for gas. Devereaux was agitated and swore that he would never let his tank fall under half ever again.

"Look at the price!" Devereaux yelled, "These bastards are soaking us for everything that they can get."

"Oil is not endless." Big Guy replied, falling back to his deep beliefs that he had formed about saving the environment and changing the world to a more sustainable place.

"This is just bullshit invented by the oil companies to pick our pockets!" Devereaux replied. Devereaux could never believe that the earth was finite; it just wasn't a part of what he knew the world to be. Big Guy thought about the article that he had read about cars that ran on alternative fuels.

"We need to get away from fossil fuels," Big Guy replied.

"Oh they've got oceans of oil!" Devereaux roared.

Big Guy smiled as if he knew what was in store for them in the future.

After filling his tank and paying for the gas, Devereaux drove back home jabbering to himself about the high cost of fuel and how the oil companies had always been crooks. He did not like the idea of being vulnerable to the whims of the powerful in our society. After all, he had been born an American and was therefore free of the control of those who would reign over him like royalty.

By the end of the week Devereaux had purchased a used 50 gallon gas tank out of a Winnebago Motor Home. He took it to a mechanic and had it installed in the bed of the pickup truck behind the cab.

"We're not going to run out of gas now," Devereaux said with a smile.

Big Guy looked at the large black metal fuel tank and replied, "Probably won't run out of gas, but if we ever get into a crash, we will go off like a roman candle."

By the end of June it was time for Big Guy and Devereaux to head north once again. After loading up the Ford Pickup and kissing Priscilla good bye, they headed north on the 405 freeway, then Interstate 5 until they had cleared the Grapevine.

Big Guy always breathed a sigh of relief when they reached the San Joaquin Valley, leaving the Los Angeles Basin behind. To Big Guy there was something depressing about Southern California. Perhaps it was the thought of what it could have been, before the wars and the Great Depression.

To Big Guy it was a place that was out of place, where the displaced came to find themselves remade according to an image that existed only in their own minds.

"How would you like to see the real Humptulips Big Guy?" Devereaux asked.

"Sure!" Big Guy replied.

By this time Interstate 5 had been completed between Bakersfield and Stockton, California. The only problem was that there were not many gas stations built along the new stretch of freeway then.

Devereaux managed to stop at a gas station in Buttonwillow to fill up his new big gas tank. As the gas pump read 60 gallons and stopped, Devereaux looked at Big Guy and winked. It was as if he had pulled off a great feat against John D Rockefeller himself.

Devereaux paid the attendant and before long they were heading north on a seemly endless ribbon of fresh white concrete.

In each direction was rolling, grass covered hills that were punctuated occasionally with clumps of brightly colored orange California Poppies. As the freeway neared a rise, one could look down on the California Aqueduct and the patchwork of green fields beyond.

Two days later Devereaux and Big Guy were traveling north on Interstate 5 in Western Washington, when Devereaux turned to Big Guy and asked, "How would you like to tour the Olympia Brewery?"

Big Guy replied, "That sounds great! Will they let me taste some beer?"

"Probably not," Devereaux replied. "But they might give you some pop instead."

It was not long before Devereaux pulled the pickup truck into the parking lot of the Olympia Brewery. At the top of the brewery, various pipes spewed an aromatic steam into the morning air. The white steam carried the smell of boiling hops and grain over the green landscape as it mixed with the morning fog to form a wonderful hybrid aroma of fresh evergreens and beer.

Once inside the brewery Devereaux and Big Guy joined a tour that began in the lobby where a young tour guide pointed out the various stages of the brewing process.

As they climbed a series of metal steps, they came to a large room with several brass kettles that contained the boiling mixture of grain, hops and water. The tour guide explained the purpose of the large kettles and pointed out the various recipes of beer brewed in this facility. After viewing the large kettles, the group walked over a skywalk where one of the tourists asked how they mowed such steep slopes. To this the tour guide replied, "We lower the lawn mower down the slope with a rope and thereby cut the grass."

It was one of those interesting bits of trivia that would seem obvious, only to remain an unasked question. After crossing the skywalk, they entered a balcony that overlooked the actual bottling area. The tour guide noted that the brewery could produce several thousand cases of beer per hour.

Finally the time had come to taste the finished product. In a room that resembled a bar, the adult visitors got the opportunity to sample the beer. Big Guy had to settle for several cups of Seven Up while Devereaux downed a few cups of Oly. The Olympia Brewery no longer exists, but it always served as a unique landmark on the road to Humptulips.

After leaving the brewery Devereaux and Big Guy turned north onto Highway 101, where they soon found themselves following the Hood Canal. As they drove along Devereaux noticed a rough wooden sign that advertised for smoked salmon. They followed the sign to a roadside shack on the shore of the canal.

They walked into the shack and were greeted by an old man who looked as though he was as old as the trees. His beard was as white as snow as he puffed a large ivory pipe. It turned out that he was an old Norwegian fisherman who had spent his life on the Olympic Peninsula. The old man offered samples of smoked fish, as Devereaux jabbered away, and they both worked to fill the silence with laughter and interesting conversation.

Big Guy watched the intricate interplay of words between the two. They talked to, through and at each other as they sized each other up. Big Guy thought to himself, "This must be what it looks like when true characters meet."

After departing the shack, Devereaux commented, "Did you see Old Marbles Odin there, by yingle?"

"Who is Marbles Odin?" I asked.

"Old Marbles Odin was a Norwegian sailor on the Ajax. He wanted to get out of the Navy so bad that he use to roll several marbles around in his hand whenever he talked to you. Old Marbles thought that he could get a Section 8 by acting crazy, he was quite the fella," Devereaux said with a smile.

They soon entered Hoodsport, where Devereaux stopped at a gas station to fill his prized gas tank to the brim. As they drove off Devereaux said, "We aren't going to run out of gas this time."

They drove past rushing rivers with magical names like; the Lilliwaup, the Hamma Hamma, the Duckabush, the Dosewallips, and the Quilcene. It was a green paradise, which on this day was sunny and warm. Log trucks sped by with one or two massive logs on their bunkers, blasting the Ox-Eye Daises that lined the road as they passed.

As lunch time approached, Devereaux pulled over onto a logging road that followed the Quilcene River. In a sunny glade they feasted on smoked salmon and crackers, as Devereaux washed it down with a bottle of Rainier Beer.

Butterflies fluttered around on the warm air as Big Guy curiously eyed their every movement. As Devereaux took a nap in the cab of the truck, Big Guy wandered around the glade trying to catalog everything that he saw. It was a long mental note that formed in Big Guy's head as he identified the life around him.

Douglas Fir, Fiddle head Fern, Douglas Squirrel, Lorquin's Admiral, Tiger Swallowtail, Green Metallic Wood Borer, and so on. At sixteen years old it was as if the world was a new place to Big Guy.

He sat on a log next to the river and dazed into the current. "There was so much more to the world than his own backyard, which wasn't that big," thought Big Guy.

Soon Devereaux walked up and startled Big Guy from his daydream. "What do you think Big Guy?" He asked with a smile.

I wish I had my butterfly net," Big Guy replied.

Devereaux laughed, "You might need a license to hunt up here!"

Big Guy noted his father's ribbing and smiled.

That night they camped in a park south of a town called Sequim. It was wieners and beans on the campfire for dinner that night. In a dark grove of giant firs, they talked as the fire light danced on their faces.

"Did you have any pets when you were a kid dad?" Big Guy asked as he poked at the fire with a stick.

Devereaux thought for a moment and smiled, "I had a duck named Joe." Devereaux replied.

"Joe was one of those white ducks. I raised him from when he was a duckling. Your granddad got him from a gas station that was giving out ducklings to anyone who filled their tank at the station. The only problem was that one day old Joe started laying eggs. Joe turned out to be a Josephine." Devereaux said with a laugh.

"I use to eat Joe's eggs for breakfast. Have you ever had duck's eggs?" he asked Big Guy with a smile.

"Not me!" Big Guy replied with a sour look on his face.

"Duck eggs are strong and they have dark yellow yolks," Devereaux said as he stared into the fire and across the years.

"Old Joe- she was a good duck that followed me everywhere. I think that a dog finally killed her. She disappeared and never came back to the wood box where I kept her by the back door."

"Did you have any other pets?" Big Guy asked his father.

"I once had two Alligator Lizards that I would attach threads to and walk around the house. My sisters would shriek and run away whenever I showed up with my lizards." Devereaux said with a smile.

As Big Guy smiled back at his father it occurred to him that the two were both the youngest of their families, joined by a bond that was unique to those who are the last born. They were both the product of parents, who may have finally learned the lessons that truly mattered in the lives of their children.

By the next day they were in Port Angeles. After a quick bite to eat at the local McDonald's, the two headed off to Olympic National Park.

It was the middle of the afternoon when they arrived at the Visitor Center on Hurricane Ridge. There were people from all over the world walking the trail to the viewpoint. As Big Guy followed his dad, a family from France stopped to take pictures. Big Guy happened to catch the eye of a beautiful girl who appeared to be his same age. She smiled at Big Guy with a beautiful smile as they passed. Distracted Big Guy tripped and fell into the backside of Devereaux, who had stopped to admire the view. She laughed as she covered her mouth shyly. Big Guy cracked a somewhat awkward smile, as the two gazed at each other for a moment.

In an instant she was gone, tugged along by a little sister who was speaking French at top speed.

"Watch where you're walking Big Guy," Devereaux said as he steadied his distracted son.

As they continued down the trail in the opposite direction, Big Guy smiled to himself as he thought about the smiling French girl.

"The world was indeed a beautiful place," Big Guy thought to himself.

Of all the exhibits the one that intrigued Big Guy the most was the interpretation of the temperate North American rain forest.

"I would like to see the rain forest dad", Big Guy proclaimed.

Devereaux answered "We can spend the night there tonight if you would like."

"That would be great!" Big Guy replied.

After a few hours of exploring the area, Devereaux and Big Guy once again started their drive down the Elwah River Valley.

The Elwah River flowed clear and bright. It was lined with giant old Red Cedars that averaged eight feet in diameter at the base. It was an ancient place where the sunlight filtered down from somewhere above, resulting in a misty green illumination that seemed to permeate the air itself.

Once again Devereaux and Big Guy were driving west on Highway 101. The highway curved through deep forests and flowered meadows. Soon they rounded a curve in the road and saw a beautiful still lake before them.

Devereaux said, "That's Crescent Lake".

The highway followed the edges of the lake and Big Guy marveled at the still, green water. The lake was so still that it mirrored the sky and the large trees that surrounded it. Every so often they passed small groups of touring bicyclists, peddling their bicycles that were ladened with camping gear.

After some time they passed the Sol Duc River and several lumber mills. The wigwam burners glowed red as blue smoke filtered skyward. The smoke was like perfume as it wafted across the road.

The aromatic smell of burning cedar shavings was synonymous with the old logging towns of the Olympic Peninsula back in the 1960's and early 70s.

Log trucks were everywhere, as Devereaux pulled over several times to let them pass.

"Those guys are trying to make a living and we are just picking our noses," Devereaux said as he pulled over once again. As the log truck passed the driver blew his air horn in thanks.

It was six o'clock in the evening when Big Guy and Devereaux pulled into Forks, Washington.

Devereaux spotted an old tavern on the left side of South Forks Avenue, with an old sign that simply said, "A Family Restaurant." Outside rusty old pickup trucks filled the parking lot.

"This looks like a good place to eat." Devereaux said with a smile.

As they entered the restaurant, they saw 20 elk heads mounted on the walls, interspersed with pictures of log trucks with single logs, and other old photos of ancient loggers perched on springboards and armed with double buck whipsaws. In the rear was an old sculpted, wooden bar with brass foot rests and even spittoons.

From somewhere over in the corner an old Wurlitzer jukebox played country and western music. Devereaux's "family restaurant" turned out to be more tavern than restaurant. And while there were a few young people present, most of the clientele were loggers enjoying a beer after a hard day in the woods. Many of the loggers still had their metal hard hats on as they laughed and drank Olympia Draft Beer from large glass mugs.

Behind the bar were several neon signs advertising Lucky Lager, Olympia, Bliz Weinhard and Rainier Beer.

Lucky for Devereaux and Big Guy, there were two empty seats at the bar. Devereaux rushed over to claim the seats as Big Guy trailed behind.

As they sat down the bartender walked up and asked what Devereaux wanted to drink. Devereaux smiled and ordered a mug of Olympia from the tap.

"And how about you-what do you want shorty?" The bartender asked Big Guy.

"I'll have a root beer," Big Guy replied as if he had just come in from the woods.

Big Guy watched as tall tales were cast about and colorful language filled the air. Some of the men were discussing logging operations. Some of them were complaining about their wives or girlfriends. Some of them merely stared into their beer, as if lost in some other place. All of them reflected hard lives and wild places.

Soon the bartender arrived and placed their drinks in front of them. As Devereaux tipped back the frosted mug and Big Guy did the same, one of the loggers who were sitting beside him had struck up a conversation with Devereaux.

"Where are you from bub?" The logger asked Devereaux.

"We're from Long Beach, California", Devereaux replied.

"What brings you to Forks?" The logger asked intently.

"We like it up here. I wanted to show my son the trees." Devereaux replied.

"Is that so....well you come to the right place," the logger said with a smile.

"We got trees here....I cut down several of em today. It's a good time of year to visit, it doesn't rain as much," the logger continued.

"Do you drive a log truck?" Big Guy asked. "Me? No I run a chainsaw." the logger smiled. "I'm not handsome enough to drive a log truck," the logger continued.

"Ya see that handsome brute over there?" the logger said with a smile as he pointed to one of his workmates drinking in the corner of the bar. "He drives a log truck and just look how pretty he is, just ask him and he will tell you!" The logger went back to sipping his beer as Devereaux laughed out loud.

All of them watched the TV that was located on the edge of the bar. The national news was on and they were reporting on some student riots that were taking place on the Berkeley Campus of the University of California. Crowds of young, long haired protesters were clashing with police as clouds of tear gas filled the air.

"You see those hippies there, they should send them here to Forks, and we would take care of them. You folks in California would not have one hippie left. Do you see any hippies here? You bet you don't, that's because we know how to deal with hippies here in Forks," the Logger said with a laugh.

Devereaux and Big Guy both laughed as Devereaux added, "I bet their mother's love them."

Like the logger, Devereaux didn't care much for hippies. Come to think of it Devereaux didn't care for all sorts of people including: Southerners, Mormons, Republicans, Jehovah Witnesses, the British and the phone company. Big Guy never saw his father mistreat anyone and he never doubted that Devereaux would give the shirt off his back to help anyone who was in need. But Big Guy saw that his father's trust extended to his family and a few friends who formed a very small circle indeed.

Within an hour, Devereaux and Big Guy were on the road again. It was twilight when they turned onto the Hoh River Road. As they drove up the narrow winding road, the forest closed in around them like a green shroud. The Hoh River Valley encompassed one of the most unique temperate rain forests in the

Pacific Northwest. As they proceeded along the road Big Guy marveled at the enormous, moss covered trees that surrounded them. As the sun set they pulled into a campground and found a spot for the night.

Devereaux grilled hamburgers while Big Guy gathered some wood for a campfire. After dinner the two sat by the blazing fire as it snapped and crackled casting a flickering orange glow into the darkness of the forest. The campsites adjacent to them were vacant, which contributed to the quiet of the scene.

As the night progressed, they could look up through the canopy of the giants above and see a glowing curtain of stars delineating the universe above them.

"Just think of how long these trees have been here Big Guy?" Devereaux said in wonder.

"They must be thousands of years old." Devereaux continued.

"It makes you feel real small," Big Guy replied.

It was another night in which Devereaux and Big Guy shared a unique moment. Like so many nights spread out over his lifetime, Big Guy looked into his father's life and tried to understand the man. The two shared their thoughts and their lives on a level that was often unspoken. But just who was this unusual man who was his father?

"Big Guy do you remember the time when we were camping in the High Sierras, I can't remember where exactly now, but the whole family was there with the old travel trailer. Anyway, I had left the ice chest out on the picnic table when just before dark; I saw a black bear trying to get into our ice chest. Well your dad was not going to let that bear run away with our breakfast, so I ran outside and proceeded to chase that bear away. After a few go rounds, the bear decided that's it was time that I stopped chasing him, so that old bear turn the tables on your dad and started chasing me around the picnic table! Your mom shouted to get back in the trailer before that bear had me for dinner. I followed your mom's advice and the bear finally wandered away without our ice chest."

"I don't remember that dad," Big Guy replied.

"You must've been too young," Devereaux continued.

"Then there was the time when we were in old town Virginia City, and your Brother Larry pulled the fire alarm. I was not in the mood for paying a fine for a false alarm, so I loaded up all you kids and we left town in a hurry."

"It's too bad that I was too young to remember that, that sounds like it would have been fun to watch!", Big Guy said with a laugh.

It was midnight and the fire was reduced to a pile of embers glowing blue and orange in the fire ring. The trunks of the giant cedars dimmed as the darkness closed in on the flickering light. The sounds of the forest night filtered through the giant columns of wood around them. Somewhere in the darkness, a Great Gray Owl called out as a gentle breeze from the vast Pacific Ocean answered back, wrestling the high branches of the great forest.

Soon Devereaux and Big Guy crawled into the back of the pickup truck to fall asleep in the gentle embrace of the dark silence.

The next day they were on the road again. It was afternoon and they were heading east across White Pass in the Cascades. Mount Rainier towered to the north as they reached the summit of the pass and started down the Tieton River. Columnar basalt rose from the canyon floor to add a fort-like appearance to the landscape.

One hundred and twenty years earlier, the Cayuse Indians had out maneuvered the U.S. Army, using those same rock outcrops.

The Pacific Northwest was like that, one large panorama of history denoted by seemingly obscure topographic features.

With a small creek here and an open meadow over there, the landscape had formed the stage of a far-reaching history of multiple cultures from the Paleolithic to the present.

It was not long before they were crossing the Columbia River at Vantage, Washington where the landscape revealed a history of epic ice age floods and advancing ice sheets.

Just past the town of George, Washington Devereaux turned off Interstate 90 onto Highway 283 and headed toward the town of Ephrata. The farther they traveled the smaller and more obscure the towns became. As if time and distance conspired to slow and expand the horizon until time seemed to stand still. The horizon blurred into a blue sky that was now starting to shift to red with the setting sun.

Devereaux drove past farm implement dealers and a hardware store until he came to a flashing yellow light in the middle of town. He turned left onto Sagebrush Flats Road and headed north.

"How do you know your way around here?" Big Guy asked.

"I'm like a homing pigeon, I can always find my way back home," Devereaux said with a smile.

"You are definitely a pigeon, that's for sure," Big Guy replied with a smile.

After some wandering around, they followed a gravel road around the north end of Jameson Lake and then followed it west and finally south again until, as if by magic the familiar tin shack showed up in the headlights in front of them.

"We're here!" Devereaux exclaimed.

After a quick meal, the two settled around a small campfire as a group of coyotes yapped from the crest of a nearby hill. Big Guy could still not understand how Devereaux could find his way around on the back roads of Douglas County in the dark. The two travelers sat close together and stared quietly into the fire, under brilliant stars that shimmered above the wide-open expanse of the Waterville Plateau.

Devereaux hugged his son as Big Guy laid his head on his father's shoulder. It was a moment that was to resonate in his memory for the rest of his life.

As the 1970's passed and Big Guy matured, his relationship with his father continued to be close. It was the spring of 1975 when Big Guy had met his future wife Sherry. Vietnam had fallen to the Communists and the energy crisis continued to wreak havoc on the world economy. Devereaux started to show his age, as his knees grew sore and he began to slow down.

At his high school, Big Guy was surrounded by the fallout that rapid change had wrought upon a fragmented society. He was bored with the predictable stereotypes that his classmates had become. During those days Big Guy believed that everyone his age was either high on pot and/or caught up in a fatalistic interpretation of a fundamentalist Jesus that he had rejected earlier in his life.

The traffic of the Los Angeles Basin droned on as Big Guy increasing sought refuge at Bolsa Chica Beach. At the beach Big Guy could turn his back on the noise of the city and look out toward the west, upon a vast and open new world. The Meehan's had been looking west for over 200 years. Perhaps somewhere beyond the sunset, their restlessness could be quenched.

Somehow Big Guy was not going to live in the world that existed behind him; the world that his father had settled for. It was Priscilla who sensing restlessness in her son, always reminded Big Guy that no matter where one ended up, they had to "take themselves with them". To Big Guy taking himself along was not a problem; the problem was in finding the way forward.

Big Guy joined the Sierra Club so that he could go hiking and learn how to rock climb. Most weekends he could be found up in the

San Gabriel Mountains or at the rocks at Rubidoux. The more he got outdoors, the more determined Big Guy was to make a living that did not depend upon a large city.

In November of 1976 Big Guy turned eighteen years old. After getting his driver's license, Devereaux offered to sell the VW to his son. It was then that he realized the meaning of being "of age" and all the opportunities that legal maturity bestowed upon those who were willing to dream and work hard towards a goal. At once Big Guy started to research job openings with any natural resource agency that he could find.

Since he was fifteen, Big Guy had always been successful at finding employment. He paid regular visits to the employment office during his lunch break from delivering flowers, a job which allowed him to drive all over the Los Angeles area.

One day while Big Guy was scanning the help wanted notices at the employment office, he found a notice that said "Seasonal Firefighter". As Big Guy read the particulars he grew more excited. The California Division of Forestry was looking for wildland firefighters and Big Guy planned on being one of those hired for the 1977 fire season. In addition to this notice, he found job openings for park rangers, wildlife biologists and other outdoor jobs. Big Guy applied for them all, as if he was an adult and not still in high school.

In March of 1977 Big Guy traveled north to Mariposa, where he took the test to become a seasonal firefighter with the California Division of Forestry.

The test included a battery of physical tests such as carrying fire hose and ladders, as well as an oral interview. Big Guy was exhausted as he drove the 250 miles back to Long Beach. Now the only thing left to do was wait.

His first success came in April of 1977 when Big Guy received a letter from the California Department of Parks and Recreation. It instructed him to report for an interview at Huntington State Beach. Within a week Big Guy was happily cleaning toilets at Bolsa Chica State Beach, one of his favorite places in Southern California.

Every so often he would still go down to the harbor with Devereaux and they would observe the passing ships, including the local Coast Guard cutters.

"I would like to join the Coast Guard", Big Guy told his father.

"While the USCG could provide for a good living, you could be stuck here", Devereaux replied.

Devereaux was right, the Coast Guard was an honorable institution in the port towns where they were stationed, and however one could not be certain of where they would be stationed.

Big Guy stared at the cutter as it bobbed next to the dock.

"Or maybe the Forest Service," Big Guy continued.

It was at moments like this that Big Guy's confidence started to waver and his deepest fears started to surface. What if he WAS stuck here? What if he could never escape Southern California? What if his life became the stereotype that he so feared?

"You will be whatever you set your mind to become. Just remember- it's like an old Jew told me one time, it's not how much money you make-it's how you spend it". Devereaux said.

It was May when Big Guy received the letter from the California Division of Forestry.

"Congratulations Firefighter- please report for duty on June 1st at the Mariposa Headquarters."

The summer of 1977 turned out to be one of the worst fire seasons in California history. Wildfires temper a young person and have served to provide a rite of passage for young westerners for generations. It was a defining period in Big Guy's life that provided clarity and purpose.

After the fire season, Big Guy sold the old VW and purchased a Ford pickup truck. It was sad to see the old VW drive away. Devereaux and Big Guy shared many good memories in that car. While the pickup was better suited to Big Guy's needs, the monthly payments proved to be a burden.

Big Guy was working at a cabinet factory, shipping finished wood to sailboat manufacturers. He was struggling to find a clear path out of Southern California, and his prospects were not promising at that time. He mailed applications out to any opening that he could find.

In March of 1978 he even took the electrical apprenticeship test up in Wenatchee, Washington. It was mostly intended to impress Devereaux; however Big Guy could see the benefits of using the family trade to escape Los Angeles.

While in Wenatchee, Big Guy visited the employment office and discovered an opening with the Washington State Parks.

When Big Guy arrived back home, he traded his pickup truck in for a VW Camper Bus.

Meanwhile Big Guy was also trying to rescue his girlfriend Sherry from a future that was even more uncertain than his own. The Meehan family history was filled with early marriages and with his prospects being what they were; Big Guy determined that Sherry and he should get married. The wedding was planned for early June as the young couple prepared for their life in Southern California.

They rented an apartment on Ball Road, in the heart of the Orange County suburbs. Big Guy was starting to feel the pull of fate on his life as he started to glumly accept his developing situation. Two days before the wedding a letter arrived in the mail, it was from the Washington State Parks.

"Congratulations, we are pleased to offer you a position at Alta Lake State Park for the 1978 field season". The letter offered Big Guy his last option for changing the course of his life, even if the position was nothing more than that of a janitor.

The day after the wedding, Big Guy and his new bride were enroute to their new life.

As Devereaux and Priscilla gave Big Guy a farewell hug, Devereaux reminded Big Guy to check the oil on the VW Bus.

So it was that Big Guy finally escaped the Los Angeles Basin to redefine his life on his own personal frontier somewhere east of a place his father called "Humptulips".

By the close of the 1970's, Big Guy and Sherry were established in the small community of Entiat, Washington. They had rented an old farm house on the banks of the

Entiat River and were living a life that neither of them could ever imagine. They kept chickens and a garden, cut firewood and worked for the U.S. Forest Service during the summer months.

But life was destined to draw Big Guy and Devereaux back together and by the latter half of the 1980's Devereaux would also be a resident of North Central Washington.

Chapter 10

Growing Older- The 1980's

The fire seasons of the 1980's started off cool and wet in the Pacific Northwest. Big Guy and his wife worked hard to make ends meet.

In the winter they worked clearing irrigation ditches and with any luck they would be hired back with the U.S. Forest Service, where they both had found temporary seasonal work ever since the summer of 1978.

Year after year they depended upon an uncertain outcome, which could have easily vaporized had it not been for hard work and a lot of luck.

As the decade continued, the summers became warmer and dryer, as frequent lightning storms ignited multiple fires at once. During this time Big Guy served on wildland fire crews where he met diverse people from all walks of life.

The fire crews of the U.S. Forest Service were unique reflections of the American People and the far- reaching vision of Teddy Roosevelt. These teams of dedicated people, who during the winter months could be Ivy League students, orchardists, loggers, restaurant workers, and a multitude of other occupations; became accomplished professional firefighters during the hot, dry months of summer.

Depending upon their training, they parachuted out of airplanes, slid down ropes from hovering helicopters, served as members of elite "hotshot" crews or served on a fire engine like Big Guy. They were some of the finest people that Big Guy had ever met.

In the rural places of the American West, the Forest Service had served as a local institution since Teddy Roosevelt first established it back in the first decade of the 20th Century. While the national government itself may as well have been located on the moon to the locals, the Forest Service Ranger Station was just down town.

Over the years Big Guy had shed much of his "city ways" and had grown to enjoy the pace and character of the small town, rural life. He had been tested by time and circumstance. Fire, floods, ice storms, sickness and injury visited him as the years passed. He had changed since he left Long Beach.

One day in the spring of 1985 Devereaux showed up unexpectedly at the front door.

"Is that you Dad?!" Big Guy exclaimed. "How is my Big Guy doing?" Devereaux boomed.

The two hugged each other as Big Guy led his father around the yard to show him the place where they lived. Sherry came out to greet her father in law and the three sat down on the sofa that sat on the back porch facing the river. They spent the morning catching up on the latest news.

After lunch Big Guy returned from doing some chores to find Devereaux stretched out, dozing peacefully on the sofa. The warm rays of the sun shined down on him as the soothing sound of the passing river enveloped him.

Big Guy stared at his father as he lay there peacefully snoozing. He was so much older than he had remembered. It had only been a year since the two had last reunited. It was then that Big Guy realized the passing of time and the fact that his father was growing old.

The next day they were off to the Sheep Ranch. The day was cold and breezy as scattered snow showers threatened. Devereaux was a little nervous as they drove up to find the tin shed partially collapsed.

"Damn- the wind knocked it over!" Devereaux exclaimed.

"Can we fix it?" Big Guy asked.

Devereaux inspected the pile of tin and wood. "No- it's too far gone", he replied.

Before long they were hiking toward Dutch Henry Draw. They hiked several miles until they found themselves standing on the cliff overlooking Moses Coulee. It was the same place where they had stood back in the summer of 1970 when the Navy Jets came screaming past. The cold wind blew hard as they stared out over the timeless landscape. Devereaux looked over at Big Guy unnoticed and smiled. It was then that Devereaux realized the passing of time and the fact that his son had become a man.

Devereaux put his arm around Big Guy and said with a smile, "I'm proud of you".

"Love you dad," Big Guy replied as the wind buffeted them both.

It was June of 1987 when Devereaux and Priscilla pulled up stakes from their life long home in Southern California and moved to East Wenatchee. Devereaux had retired as an electrician and Priscilla was anxious to move closer to her children, most of who had already moved north. Devereaux was not certain about winter in the inland Northwest. He had never encountered snow during the winter in Southern California. Big Guy always teased his father about the threat that Devereaux might get snowed in while at home in East Wenatchee and that he would be forced to resort to cannibalism like the Donner Party did in the high passes of the Sierra.

It seemed strange to Big Guy that his parents would move north. All those years that Devereaux had watched the 20th Century

refugees from the Midwest and the Dust Bowl
stream into his homeland, he could never
imagine that he would be like them one day-
searching for a new home in a strange place.
Big Guy could understand the resentment of
the locals who watched the influx of strangers
invading their familiar world. The West has
always been that way; locals making way for
newcomers and different ideas about how the
world should be. New ideas, like ripples from
pebbles tossed into a pond, have been creating
turbulence since the landing of Columbus in
the New World.

One day Big Guy was sitting on the back
porch visiting with a friend from work, when
suddenly Devereaux rode into the yard on a
small motorcycle. It was a motorcycle that he
had actually found in a trash heap. Devereaux
had been a collector of junk since he was a
child. While he wasn't a hoarder, he was
known to reuse objects that he found
discarded in his travels.

Today he was adorned in a collection of
"useful" items that, to the casual observer
would seem hilarious and somewhat strange.

Big Guy was at a loss as he turned to see his
friends' reaction to this strange, seemingly
homeless man who appeared from nowhere,
riding an undersized motorcycle while sporting
a recycled motorcycle helmet, a pair of welders

goggles, a bowling ball bag over his shoulder (just in case he needed to haul more pickings) and different colored socks on each foot.

"How are you doing Big Guy?" Devereaux bellowed.

"Fine dad-how are you today?" Big Guy replied.

Big Guy's friend was somewhat taken back by the fact that the two actually knew each other, let alone they were related.

Big Guy introduced Dave to his father, "Dad this is my friend Dave- he works with me on the fire crew".

Devereaux removed his welding goggles just long enough to acknowledge Dave.

"Glad to meet you Dave!" Devereaux replied in a booming voice.

"Well I need to fill the trash cycle up with gas before I head back home", Devereaux said as he donned his welding goggles and backed the undersized motorcycle out of the yard.

Before Big Guy could say another word, Devereaux was flying off down the driveway on his trash cycle in a cloud of dust.

Big Guy turned to Dave and said with a smile, "That's my dad."

By the summer of 1988, Big Guy had finally landed a permanent position as a fire engine captain with the U.S. Forest Service in Entiat. Life was starting to come together for Big Guy and Sherry. Just before he was dispatched to the wildfires that were burning that summer in Yellowstone National Park, Big Guy learned that he was to become a father.

At 3:30AM on February 4th, 1989 Erik Meehan came into the world. It was later that morning when Devereaux and Priscilla first held their grandson. Big Guy beamed as he watched his father hold his new grandson. It was an ancient feeling that resonated in the room that cold winter morning. Another generation had arrived to carry on the journey that started so long ago.

From then on, trips with his father became less frequent, as Big Guy's life grew more complex. Devereaux and Priscilla were getting on in years and health issues were becoming more common for both of them.

The lives of the Meehans had reached some form of stability by the time the 1980's came to a close.

Chapter 11

The 1990's

It was the end of July when after a long dry spell, a warm wind approached the town of Entiat from the Southwest. By 11:00 AM towering cumulus clouds were building to the south and west.

Big Guy, now Engine Captain Meehan, was just returning home from an assignment up north in Okanogan County, when he walked into his house to find Devereaux babysitting little Erik, while his mom was away at work.

"How are things going Dad?" Big Guy asked his father as he untied his boots and stripped off the soot covered fire shirt that he had been wearing for the past week.

"Evening in Torrance!" Devereaux exclaimed as the pungent aroma of smoke and sweat wafted across the room. Whenever anything smelled especially bad, Devereaux would refer to the City of Torrance in California as if it were some brand of perfume.

Torrance was often well known for being the unfortunate recipient of the downwind fumes of the oil refineries from Wilmington next door.

"How was my baby boy today?" Big Guy asked as he tip toed into the nursery and peeked in to see his son sleeping peacefully in his crib.

"He was swell, he only dumped his lunch twice. That little guy is almost as regular as his old grandpa," Devereaux said with a smile. In this case "dumping his lunch" could only mean one thing, and the proof was found in the missing paper diapers from his son's diaper bag.

"Thanks dad!" Big Guy replied as he made his way to the bathroom for a shower.

"Did you get that fire put out up in the Okanogan?" Devereaux asked.

"We hammered it good Dad!" Big Guy replied loudly as he stood in the warm, soothing water.

As a week's worth of dirt and soot washed away, Big Guy could feel every muscle unwind as he thought about what was for dinner that night and if his father might want to stay and eat.

Just as Big Guy was washing the shampoo out of his hair, a loud clap of thunder and a simultaneous bolt of lightning shook the house. Big Guy jumped from the shower and dried off in a hurry as he rushed to dress himself in clean fire resistant clothes. Within minutes Big Guy had retied his boots and was bolting toward the door.

"Where are you going son?" Devereaux asked as Big Guy was heading out the door.

"I think we have another fire to deal with!" Big Guy replied. The words had no more cleared his lips as he noticed a wisp of smoke above the rim of Dick Mesa, less than a mile west of the house.

"Could you please watch Erik until his mom gets home?" Big Guy asked his father.

"I can watch him- you go make a living son," Devereaux replied as he waved from the porch.

"Thanks Dad!" Big Guy shouted as he drove away towards the ranger station.

When Big Guy arrived at the ranger station, his crew members Jose and Katie were still chatting by the fire engine. Big Guy parked his pick up and hurried down to the engine.

"Are you folks ready to fight some fire?" Big Guy asked his crew.

"Do we have a fire?" Katie asked.

"Look up there," Big Guy said as he pointed towards the top of the mesa. Both crewmembers were somewhat shocked to see smoke where there was none before.

"Load up- let's go!" Big Guy shouted as they got into the fire truck and drove out of the station.

"Dispatch this is Engine 501 be advised that we are enroute to a fire above Entiat that is burning on Dick Mesa." Big Guy said as he navigated his engine through town and turned onto a dirt road that would take them to the scene of the fire.

"Engine 501 we copy that you are enroute to a fire on Dick Mesa, please provide a legal description when you get the chance," Dispatch replied.

After driving for a couple of miles up a small, brush covered canyon that terminated in the town itself, Big Guy cleared the ridge that separated the top of Dick Mesa from Auvil Canyon and the steep breaks of the Columbia River. All three firefighters were awestruck to find a single strip of windblown wildfire rushing upslope toward the road that they were on. If they could find an anchor point and run fire from that point along the road above the fire, they might be able to hold the fire to the lower slope. In essence they could use fire to fight the fire before it crossed the road.

"Dispatch we have a legal description for the Dick Mesa Fire. Township 25 North, Range 21 East, Section 8, Northeast of the Southwest Quarter. The fire is moving up slope quickly; right now we are requesting retardant, five engines and one hand crew. Please notify Chelan County that this fire might threaten the town of Entiat if we can't get a handle on it quickly," Engine 501.

Dispatch replied, "How many air tankers will you require 501?"

"As many as you can find," Big Guy replied.

"Copy that- we will see what we can do," Dispatch replied.

Big Guy headed toward the fire as he briefed his subordinates of the plan and in which direction they were to escape if things should go wrong. Big Guy was aware of the challenges associated with trying to control a fire at midslope, during midday on such a hot and unstable summer's day on the breaks of the Columbia River. However the fire had yet to gain energy and if they could deny it fuel before it reached its peak, perhaps they could keep it in check until help arrived.

"Jose I will need you to fire off the road just above the fire, keep going until I tell you to stop.

Katie, I will need you to follow close behind Jose with a charged hose. I will follow in the engine. Jose remember- a little fire will go a long way today, we just want to slow it down."

"Copy that Boss!" Jose replied with a smile.

All was going well until a log rolled down the hill below the road and ignited some heavy brush. The flames roared back up the hill until they were over fifty feet high. The fire front rolled like a wave over the road behind them, igniting the slope above.

"Jose dose your fusee, we will need to regroup.

Katie- roll up the hose we need to reposition the engine down the road," Big Guy ordered his crew members back to the engine.

"Engine 501 this is Dispatch, be advised that you are the designated Incident Commander- are you ready to copy the resources that we have enroute to your incident?"

"Copy- go ahead with that," Big Guy replied.

Dispatch continued, "2 ten-person hand crews- Natches Crew 1 and Leavenworth Initial Attack. 5 Engines- Engine 606, Engine 523, Engine 607, State Engine 22 and County Engine 781. 4 Air tankers- You have Tanker 35, Tanker 66, Tanker 67, and Tanker 55.

Big Guy jotted down the list of resources on a clipboard and replied, "Copy that Dispatch, what is the possibility of getting a helicopter, some more air tankers and a Type 2 Incident Management Team? We have a developing situation here. The fire has jumped the Dick Mesa Road and is heading up slope. It's spreading out on all sides and will be cresting the ridge just west of Entiat. There's a good chance that it will head into town through Auvil Canyon as the evening downslope breeze kicks in." Big Guy paused and then asked, "Dispatch, this is Dick Mesa IC- did you copy?"

Dispatch replied, "Dick Mesa IC, we copy and will see if Montana and Idaho can send us any more air tankers. Be advised that Air Attack 02 will be over your fire in 45 minutes, and the ETA for Lead Plane 62 and Air Tanker 35 is 15 minutes."

Big Guy replied, "Copy that dispatch-thank you, Dick Mesa IC."

By this time the fire was rapidly spreading in all directions, making it difficult for Big Guy to prioritize where to place the incoming retardant first. Several minutes later County Engine 781 arrived and started to attack the eastern edge of the fire from the road. Engine 501 had repositioned itself on the west side of the fire so as to serve as a command post.

Soon Big Guy heard a scratchy voice coming over the radio. "Dick Mesa IC, this is Lead 62, what are your wishes?"

Big Guy replied, "Lead 62 we need to prevent this fire from rolling into town through that small canyon on the east side of the fire. Could you lay down some retardant in that gap at the top of the canyon so as to keep the fire out of there?"

After a short time and a few revolutions above the fire, the lead plane pilot replied, "So put the mud across the top of this small canyon at my three o'clock?"

"That is correct Lead 62, we want to keep the fire out of town," Big Guy replied.

The Lead Plane Pilot replied, "Lead 62 copies that, we will see what we can do."

Before Big Guy could reply, the lead plane pilot asked, "Is that you down there in the drop zone?"

"Negative 62, I'm on the west side." Big Guy replied.

"Copy that Dick Mesa IC, be advised that we can't drop with that engine in the area," replied the lead plane pilot. Big Guy realized that County Engine 781 was in the drop zone as he tried to call the engine on the radio to clear the area. It was apparent that Big Guy was not able to communicate with the county engine; it was an ongoing problem that different fire departments had problems with the ability to communicate across frequencies. Judging from the present situation with the county engine, it would not be too long before they would be forced to abandon their position anyway. The fire had swept past the county engine and continued its march toward town.

"Lead 62, do you see this wheat field over here on the west side?" Big Guy asked.

"Copy that Dick Mesa IC, we see that," replied the lead plane pilot.

"Could you drop a line down slope from the top so as to cut off the western flank from reaching that wheat field?" Big Guy replied.

"I copy that, Lead 62."

Just then Big Guy saw a large, four engine, propeller-driven aircraft appear over the fire. It was an old converted DC-7 aircraft that circled high overhead. Big Guy cleared Engine 501 out of the drop zone as the fire roared headlong toward the wheat field. Soon the Lead Plane swooped in over the ridge to the north with its landing lights flashing in an alternating pattern. It was followed by the loud roar of engines attached to a shining red belly tank that opened as the air tanker neared the ridge. 1,000 gallons of bright red retardant fell toward the edge of the flames as the aircraft passed overhead. It fell as a cascading mist, like a life giving spring had opened in the sky above the fire.

Big Guy was staring at the results of the drop when he looked up to see Earl Shadwick, who had served many years as a Fire Management Officer in the area. Big Guy had worked for Earl for many years, before Earl had retired a few years earlier. Now here was old Earl standing next to his pickup truck in a pair of red sneakers, asking Big Guy how things were going.

"Things are going great Earl!" Big Guy replied with a smile. "What brings you up here?"

"Just figured that I would come up here and see how you were getting along," Earl replied as he inspected the retardant drop.

"Why are you putting retardant there?" Earl asked.

It seemed an inopportune time to discuss tactics with the old man, but Big Guy humored the old coot with the best answer that he could muster. "I think that if the fire gets into this wheat field it will be off to the races- up the hill, over the ridge and into town before you know it," Big Guy replied.

"You won't need to worry about the wheat field Partner," Earl replied with a smile.

Just then the fire outflanked the retardant line and slammed into the wheat field with great intensity, only to die out after burning 10 feet into the field.

Big Guy looked at Earl in astonishment, "How did you know that? That wheat field stopped that fire cold. I think that I can actually use it as a fire line!" Big Guy shouted excitedly.

"I fought this fire back in '62, this wheat isn't fully cured, it's still green toward the base," Earl said with a smile as he jumped into his pickup and drove away toward town. Big Guy thought about it and noticed that the wheat was still green near the ground.

"Dick Mesa IC this is Lead 62, where do you want the rest of Tanker 35's load?"

"Lead 62- concentrate your drops on top of the ridge and down that canyon that leads into town," Big Guy replied.

By this time the fire had grown to over 900 acres. By this time the wildfire was creating a large column of smoke that blocked out the sun over the town of Entiat. Back at Big Guy's home, Devereaux was excitedly pacing back and forth as the smoke started to billow over the ridge just west of the house. Erik started to cry in the nursery as the smoke filtered through his open window. Devereaux came into the house and started to close the windows, before picking up his grandson and cuddling him on his large shoulders.

One by one the engines were arriving on scene as Big Guy briefed each one and assigned them a mission, radio frequencies and safety instructions.

Soon the hand crews arrived and they were also briefed and assigned to an area of fire line. Line supervision soon arrived and order ruled the western flank of the fire.

Big Guy looked up to see eight air tankers orbiting overhead. Above the orbit of the air tankers he could see an air attack plane that served as the conductor of this symphony of flying metal. As he drove back toward Auvil Canyon Big Guy could see a wall of flames funneling down the canyon toward town. Just then the lead plane swooped in with three air tankers in tow. As the retardant fell like rain, Big Guy continued down the canyon, beating the flames into town. By this time the town was in total chaos.

Civilians were loading pickups with their belongings, as local fire departments had fire engines stationed at strategic locations around town. Big Guy stopped to chat with a Sheriff's deputy that he knew well. The deputy was somewhat overwhelmed as another air tanker came screaming in overhead, dumping its gooey red load into the edge of town and through the open windows of the deputy's patrol car.

"Dick Mesa IC this is Air Attack 02, I wanted to inform you that you will be losing all of your air tankers with the exception of Tanker 35. We just broke a large fire down in Central Oregon that is threatening homes. You can use 35 for one more run, and then you will lose him too...Air Attack 02."

"Dick Mesa IC copies," Big Guy replied.

Big Guy stopped by the ranger station to see if he could borrow a pickup so that he could free up his engine to better engage the fire.

Lucky for him Kyle Wallace, an assistant engine captain from Engine 425 who was called in from his days off, was available to take command of Engine 501.

Big Guy soon found a pickup truck that belonged to the timber crew. He jumped in and noticed that the fire had come over the ridge above his house and was blowing downhill towards Devereaux and his son. Big Guy suddenly realized the gravity of the situation and raced off to warn his dad.

When he arrived back at the house Big Guy found Devereaux carrying little Erik around in his arms, as he nervously watched the flames get closer to the house.

"Am I ever glad to see you!" Devereaux exclaimed as he met Big Guy in the driveway. They gave each other a hug as Big Guy took his son into his arms.

"I was about to take little Erik and split!" Devereaux said excitedly. "I've never been this close to a hillside that was on fire before."

Before Big Guy could answer the radio crackled, "Dick Mesa IC this is Lead 62, where do you want this final load?"

"Lead 62, if you could split your load over here on the north east side of the fire I would appreciate that," Big Guy spoke into his radio as he winked at his father.

Devereaux suddenly realized that it was his youngest son who was managing the chaos around him. He watched every move that Big Guy made and everything that he said. In one arm Big Guy held his son and in the other a two way radio. Devereaux noticed that his son was as calm as if he was walking on the Sheep Ranch on a spring morning. In those smoky moment's time slowed, as events that stretched out over a lifetime came into focus. Devereaux could see the sun shining on the ocean of his youth, as he tossed his youngest boy into the sky and over the waves that rolled turbulent into the shore.

Big Guy pointed to a ridge to the north of the house where a line of flames was backing through the cheat grass and sage brush. As he whispered into the ear of his precious little son, a large aircraft appeared over the flaming ridge, being led by a smaller aircraft in front of it. The smoke parted into multiple vortices' from the slipstream of the large wings and radial engines. The tanks on the large plane opened and the retardant rained down along the fire's edge clear on past where the three were watching. Erik giggled wildly as the large aircraft thundered by overhead.

Devereaux could only stare in wonder as Big Guy turned to him and smiled. The flames hissed and diminished as the forward spread was checked.

As Big Guy organized a few more incoming resources, he hugged his boy and his father before heading off in the pickup to continue the mission at hand.

Late that evening, Big Guy tip toed quietly into the small house, where his wife and son were sleeping soundly. He sat for a moment in the kitchen staring out at a patch of glowing embers on the hillside above the house. Big Guy tugged on his boots until, one by one; they slipped off to reveal the retardant stained socks inside. Big Guy sat there at the kitchen table- wiggling his toes as he studied the stack of mail that filled a shoe box there. After thumbing through the bills, Big Guy stood up stiffly and headed off to take a shower, before heading off to bed for the night.

In the morning Big Guy awoke to the sound of a soft rain falling on the roof. He walked outside to find the fire from yesterday cold on the blackened hillside behind his house.

Within two years Big Guy and Sherry moved to Sutherlin, Oregon. Sherry had landed a promotion with the US Bureau of Land Management or the BLM as it is known in the West. Big Guy thought that it would be a good idea to assist with his wife's personal development. It was a difficult move for Big

Guy, as he had to reel back his own career. He loved the Entiat Valley. But it was he who nudged his wife to accept the job, and early in June of 1991 they packed up their belongings and left the only place they had ever lived after getting married in 1978.

By the time August had arrived fire season was in full swing. Big Guy had managed to get a position working in the BLM fire warehouse in Roseburg. It was not too long before Big Guy felt isolated from his firefighting career. While he was qualified to manage large wildfires, Big Guy found himself handing out shovels and canteens. Life was not going too well in this new place and he missed the dry, pine covered canyons of the east side of the Cascade Mountains.

In October of that year Big Guy's second son, Sam was born. It was rough at first, as Sam came into the world with complications. Over time Sam thrived as Big Guy began to focus more on his family.

After four years Big Guy had managed to get back into fire suppression. He even received a promotion to a fire operations specialist at Roseburg. However when an opportunity came to apply for a fire position on the "East Side" he jumped at it. As the spring of 1995 arrived, Big Guy found himself serving as the manager of a remote fire station on the Crooked River east of Prineville, Oregon.

Devereaux and Priscilla had moved to Vancouver, Washington to be closer to the doctors and the Kaiser medical facility that was located there. Both were growing old and they were beginning to experience chronic health issues. They moved into a nice house on the corner of Northeast 14th in Vancouver. Life continued with a few more bumps for Devereaux and Priscilla. They had survived so much together over the years and now they were struggling with the challenges of age. While they considered that their relationship had never been what could be described as blissful, they still loved each other- in spite of themselves.

Before Big Guy had moved to Central Oregon and Devereaux was in better health, the two once again hit the road. This time it was in a Ford Pickup truck, with an old camper attached that Devereaux had found in the classified ads. It was a Friday morning in April when Devereaux pulled into the yard in Sutherlin and declared that the journey should begin immediately. The destination was the old mining camp in the desert of Arizona near the foot of the Superstition Mountains where one hundred years earlier, his mother Ethel

Meehan had killed rattlesnakes and battled wild Havelinas.

By dark they were parked in a wide spot northwest of Winnemucca, Nevada watching the moon rise over the dark desert. While coyotes howled and a cold breeze rustled the sagebrush around them, both were quiet as they stared at the vast ceiling of stars that crowded the black sky above.

Sunrise in the Great Basin can be magical.

That morning was one of those stunning displays that live on in one's mind long after the years have passed. The light started slowly at first, then it streamed forth from the clear horizon, turning purple and orange as it beamed in a gleaming crescent from the east. A slight breeze blew across Big Guy's face as he turned to watch the light reflected in his father's own weathered face. Big Guy had never noticed the old lines that etched Devereaux's face before that moment. It was as if the morning light had revealed his father as a mere mortal, fearful and feeling alone in the world. Big Guy began to feel sad as he took note of the passing years in the span of a second. Could it all come to an end so soon- in the wink of an eye?

After breakfast in Winnemucca, they were making good progress along Interstate 80 and discussing everything from politics to religion.

Devereaux was making some point about interracial marriage and made some derogatory comment in which the word "Nigger" featured prominently. It was the final straw for Big Guy as he had grown tired of all the times in his life that he had heard that word bantered about by his father and brothers.

"Damn it dad- you sound like some ignorant red neck!" Big Guy was surprised that his complaint had rolled so easily off his tongue.

"I'm sick and tired of you using that term to describe a whole race of people who you don't even know!" Big Guy exclaimed.

Devereaux looked over at Big Guy with a look of mild surprise. He had spent a lifetime denigrating all sorts of people and no one had ever called him on it. It was one of the parts of this complex man that was a reflection of the geography and history in which he had lived. Yet here was his last born son, challenging him on this one foregone fragment that had survived all the challenges of the recent decades.

"I'm still your dad!" Devereaux snapped back as he focused on the road and the increasing speed that he found himself demanding from the gas pedal. There was an uneasy silence for a few hundred miles as the Bonneville Salt Flats came and went in a blur.

After filling up with gas at a roadside station, the two stopped for dinner at a small diner across the street. Devereaux and Big Guy sat down in a booth next to the window as a flock of seagulls landed in the parking lot outside.

"Look at the seagulls out there, they are the national birds of Utah," Devereaux said with a smile. "Seagulls saved the Mormons by eating grasshoppers, so they put one on top of the temple in Salt Lake."

Big Guy looked at his father and shook his head. "You are as full of bull as a peach orchard owl dad!" Big Guy said with a smile.

"At least my mother loves me," Devereaux replied.

They spent that night in a rest area south of Cedar City. As he tossed and turned in the cramped camper, Big Guy looked over to see his father on his back snoring like a foundered mule. There was something different about this trip, something final that suggested that the future would be different. Big Guy sensed that something was not right with his father. Devereaux had been impatient and somewhat agitated during the whole trip. The two were increasingly tense as the trip progressed. By the time they had reached Superior, Arizona at the foot of the Superstition Mountains, Devereaux was not in a very good mood. To Big Guy he seemed tired and out of sorts. The two sat in the camper on a side street discussing the life that his mother had lived in those foreboding mountains above the town. Devereaux could not remember how to get back into the Silver King town site where his mother Ethel had grown up all those years ago. It was then that he turned to Big Guy and said, "It's time to head back home."

Big Guy looked at his father in wonder and asked, "You want to go home?"

"But we just got here!" Big Guy exclaimed. "It's time to go home," Devereaux replied.

With that he started the camper up and off they went back in the direction in which they had come. By days end they were south of Flagstaff, where they spent the night in a rest area that overlooked a canyon. As Big Guy lay there, staring at the ceiling of the camper, he grew more apprehensive about his father's health. Big Guy knew that he would not get any more info from his father on the subject of his father's health so he didn't press the subject.

By the time Devereaux and Big Guy arrived back in Oregon, both realized that they had traveled far enough together for a while.

Chapter 12

The Unbroken Circle

Paulina Fire Station was indeed a lonely spot on the banks of the Crooked River, a high desert tributary which appears out of an opening in the basalt and flows west across the wide open spaces of Central Oregon. Big Guy spent his days alone, preparing the station for the upcoming fire season.

The wind blew cold, as dark clouds glided across the sky toward Big Summit Prairie. The afternoon shadows were growing long, when a Ford Pickup came roaring into the compound.

It was Devereaux and he was smiling from ear to ear like a Cheshire cat as Big Guy came out onto the porch to greet him.

"How's my Big Guy doing?" Devereaux enthusiastically asked as he hugged his son.

"Not bad dad for a young, tender pigeon", Big Guy replied with a smile.

It was as if the two had picked up right where they had left off so long ago. Soon the stories were flowing like all those rivers they had experienced together over the years. Devereaux had brought the goodies, including steaks, baked potatoes and beer.

As the setting sun broke through the clouds on the western horizon, the haunting calls of a

Common Snipe drifted in from the reeds along the river. Orange light bathed the twisted Juniper trees that casted strange shadows across the distant basalt canyons.

Devereaux raised a beer as if to toast the fading light, as Big Guy finished the last of his bottle. The two sat silently as if in a church. Perhaps they were. It was a form of worship that celebrated each other's presence and the lives that were common to them both. Big Guy looked at his father and found an old man enjoying the simple things, like a cold beer and a solid porch on the edge of a river out West. The moment was sublime and both of them sensed it.

The wind blew across Devereaux's weathered face as a slight smile formed. Tears welled up in Devereaux's eyes as he said, "I'm proud of you Big Guy. This is a beautiful place and you have done well."

They were tears of happiness formed by a good man who could not express the joy of a life well lived. A life that he knew was soon to be finished.

As the darkness came and the stars appeared, the two gazed up at the starlight cascading down from above. "Thanks Dad." Big Guy said as he put his arm around his father and hugged him.

It was the last time that Devereaux and Big Guy would share a moment together on the open expanses of the American West.

It was the late winter of the year 1997 and Devereaux was fading fast. He was dying from kidney failure and would not listen to the pleas of his family to seek dialysis. Devereaux swore that he would never be dependent upon a machine and the hospitals in which those machines exist. It was the trademark of a generation that had survived the Great Depression and the horrors of World War II. It was also the trademark of a unique man who deeply feared the prospect of being locked away; forgotten, helpless and alone.

Devereaux's time was growing short as members of his family arrived to keep a vigil.

One afternoon while Big Guy was taking a nap in another room, he awoke to hear his brother Steve speaking to Devereaux. Devereaux was struggling to breathe and Steve was there by his side, telling him to "just let go".

There was Devereaux, fighting death at the very end and his eldest son, Steve. Steve was the one son that he had the most issues with. It was Steve who was the one by his side in the end. Big Guy had made up his mind that he was not going to see his father like that; he lacked the courage to see his father suffer.

After a few moments Devereaux relaxed and followed Steve's advice. Devereaux had passed on his own terms, as he had wanted his life to end.

A few years later Steve died and two years afterward Priscilla died as well.

Big Guy knew that we all end up as orphans. Loss is the price that life exacts of us for the good times that we shared with the people that we hold dear.

****

In the autumn of 2002 Big Guy brought his two sons to the Sheep Ranch, where they sat around a campfire at night and talked about the world around them. They slept under a blanket of stars and listened to the Coyotes howl from over in Dutch Henry Draw. The old stories were told as the three of them enjoyed each other's company and all was right with their world.

The circle was unbroken and the passing of time continued as it had since the words were passed from the first father to his son, in a world that was continually renewed by the telling.

The End.